THE PRINCE AND THE PIE MAKER

THE REBEL ROYALS BOOK 2

SHANAE JOHNSON

THOSE JOHNSON GIRLS

The duck was overcooked, though no one mentioned it. Instead, every dinner guest continually raised their forks to their mouths with polite grimaces of appreciation. The potatoes were seasoned well-enough with pimentón. Although at the center, a few spuds were raw. The greens had been braised in a sauce peppered with azafrán and comino. But many stalks were soggy.

The Spanish spices hadn't hidden the flaws. Especially not for a palate that had savored the paprika fruit straight from the vine in its native land of Mexico. Furthermore, the strong metallic notes of the saffron hinted that the flowers had been harvested far from its Mediterranean roots. And the cumin seeds, which had a distinct warming flavor when plucked from its native soil in Iran, were decidedly lukewarm.

The visiting Catalonian chef puffed up his chest as though he'd made a meal fit for a king. In truth, the King of Cordoba wore a smile that said he quite enjoyed the meal. But for the second son of Cordoba, the meal lacked a certain innovation and fusion that the worldly prince had grown accustomed to.

Prince Alexander had traveled the world over in search of the perfect bite of food. There wasn't a plant he hadn't tried, a spice he couldn't stomach, nor a part of an animal he wouldn't take a bite out of. Alex's years of culinary adventure and exploration had been the envy of, and later the model of, the likes of a certain travel chef that also had no reservations.

The fare at the palace state dinner was fine, which was great for fine dining. But Alex knew that food could be an adventure. Too bad he wasn't let into the castle's main kitchen. From an early age, his parents had frowned at his culinary skill and later outright banned him from the scullery. Sitting at the dining table as the doors to the kitchen opened and closed Alex felt like a duck. On the surface, he was calm, cool, and collected; the perfect prince charming for the guests seated around him. But, if anyone poked their head beneath the surface, they'd see his foot tapping out an anxious rhythm.

Alex wanted to return to the small kitchenette in his wing of the castle and grab a few ingredients. With his spices in tow, he wanted to go into the main kitchen and add a dash of cane sugar to the potatoes. He wanted to replace the water in the pot of greens with grapeseed oil to compliment the warm notes of the saffron and cumin. He wished he could've taken the meat out just a few minutes early.

But he couldn't. He wouldn't. Just like the tough skin on the duck, Alex had learned to toughen up and hide behind a brawny exterior that sheltered a complex interior.

The clinking of glasses brought Alex's attention around. He watched as his brother, King Leonidas stood to address his gathered guests.

Like Alex, Leo was dressed in partial regalia. A suit and his sash and medals, but not his crown. The royals only brought that out for formal events, and this was just one of many state dinners.

Alex's presence wasn't mandatory. He'd come because he wanted to try the fare of the Spanish chef. So far, he was underwhelmed and wished he'd stayed upstairs and prepared his own meal.

"It has been a momentous couple of months for our great nation," said Leo. "We have forged a new partnership that has already put many Cordovians back to work."

Leo nodded to the Spanish Duchess who had almost been Alex's new sister-in-law. Lady Teresa smiled back at her almost-been fiancé. Though she hadn't gained a crown, Lady Teresa had no hard feelings. Her partnership with the country would net her millions, and that was far more of a dream come true than marrying royalty for a modern woman such as her.

Leo turned to his right and gazed down at the love of his life. "And soon, I will solidify my greatest partnership, and Cordoba will have a new queen."

Esme gazed back up at her fiancé, the same look of love in her eyes. The two looked at each other as though they were a three course dessert meal.

Far from what was believed of him, the sight of true love didn't turn Alex's stomach. His heart was overjoyed to see his brother in such a state of bliss. It just wasn't something Alex ever cared to experience for himself.

He could never understand having the same meal twice in a row. So why would he ever have the same woman more than once? There were so many new dishes to try, new food combinations to mix, new spices to add to the side dishes. It would take a lifetime to try them all, and that's exactly what Alex wanted to do with his life. Spice it up every day.

"And here's to my future husband," said Esme, "the love of my life, the slayer of dragons, the king of my dreams brought into reality."

There was an uncomfortable clearing of throats around the room. Royals and dignitaries weren't accustomed to showing emotion in public. But Esme was neither royal nor Cordovian. One of the many reasons Alex liked her so much. That and her flairs for the colorful, fairytale dramatics she brought into the once starch-white palace.

"Hear, hear." Alex raised his glass and spoke into the wary silence.

Leo chuckled and followed suit. He clinked glasses with the queen of his heart and sipped, never taking his eyes off her. Soon, the others around the table raised their glass to the unconventional toast.

Esme was growing on the country. She'd visited a school and publicly gave advice. But instead of being affronted, the teachers actually listened to her ideas. Penelope was entirely in love with her soon to be stepmother, and the two were often gallivanting about the castle looking for fairies or other nonsensical creatures in the corners. Alex joined them a time or two and had great fun. But what he loved most about his new family member was the smile Esme put on his brother's often serious face.

Yes, Esme was good for the country. She was changing things for the better. Forcing people to update their views on how things should be done and what could be. Unfortunately, Esme's perceptions hadn't colored every part of the kingdom.

"I'm surprised you've been here so long, your highness," said the Duke of Ebra. "You're typically off at some party or concert with a super model or two."

That wasn't entirely false. Alex did party but typically when said party was at a restaurant with a dish he wanted to try. Concerts were less his thing. It was more and more the food trucks parked outside the concerts that were Alex's jam. He'd stopped dating supermodels years ago when they demurred from wanting to go out to restaurants and try fat-filled, full cream, carb-loaded dishes without substitutions. Alex loathed any diner with the gall to ask a chef to change his or her vision for the food put on the plate.

The duke continued without waiting for Alex's reply. Few people were actually interested in his replies. Most had a prescribed opinion of the Prince of Cordoba, and they had no interest in substitutions where Alex was concerned.

"You must be glad your brother has found a bride," said the duke. "Otherwise, the duties of state would've fallen to you if he had no male heir."

"That is a rule my brother is looking to change," said Alex. "Gender will no longer be a requirement of succession. So, the country is quite safe from my rule."

The duke jerked back with distaste at the announcement. He looked down the table to where Leo leaned over and spoke into Esme's ear. "Still, I suppose you will be marrying soon, regardless. Your brother can change the laws of succession, but he can't change the terms of your inheritance."

"Who shall the lucky girl be?" The Viscount of Jucar joined in on the conversation.

"I had believed Lady Brie of Baetica was your intended," said the duke.

Alex carved a piece of the duck and placed it into his mouth. Still as chewy as dry steak. He reached past his wine glass for his mug and sipped his tea. He knew he wasn't needed for the conversation.

People talked about him. People talked over him. People talked behind his back all his life.

No one bothered to find out what he really thought, what he actually did, or who he truly was. It was far more interesting to categorize him as the playboy prince or the restless spare. It was a role thrust upon him by the media. He'd been content to play it so long as it afforded him a place at the various tables around the world where he could try new and exciting dishes. The attention from the women hovering about his chair was nice, so long as they didn't interrupt until the last bite.

The talk about him continued around the table. As always, Alex wasn't interested. His attention was on the chocolate dessert being placed on the table. Just one whiff of the sweet concoction and he was disappointed. He knew before he bit into it that the moist block of cake that it would be a saccharin soiree.

Sugar needed a partner to temper it. He wished the cook had added cayenne to the dessert. It would've given it a mighty and unexpected kick. Alex had learned that trick from an unassuming baker. Her food had packed a punch; a punch he could still taste on the tip of his tongue.

Jan had been the only chef whose dish he'd wanted to try again and again. It was because she added another spice to her leftovers before the second helping. She'd be back in a few weeks for the wedding festivities. Esme had insisted that her best friend bake the pies for the wedding. Alex's mouth watered in anticipation.

Alex pushed the dessert to the side. "Would you gentlemen excuse me?"

Everyone around him nodded but made no plea for him to stay. No one expected him to sit still. They expected him to go off and make a ruckus that they would read about in tomorrow's papers and then say they were with him before it happened.

"Where are you off to?" asked Leo as Alex made his way toward the exit.

"Devilry and debauchery are calling, so I must heed it."

Leo shook his head but said nothing. Alex knew that Leo was the one soul he could count on in this world. But he also knew that even Leo couldn't see, or simply wasn't interested in, Alex's true nature.

Esme reached out and opened her arms to Alex. Alex went willingly, uncaring of the unfashionable display of emotion that royals were not supposed to engage in. Hugging his soon to be sister-in-law in front of a room of dignitaries would be frowned on. Which should have been reason enough for Alex to do it. But he simply liked the affection Esme showed openly.

"Don't burn anything down." She winked at him.

He'd only known Esme for a month. But he was certain the former teacher knew exactly what he was up to.

"I make no promises," he said, giving her a peck on

the cheek.

He didn't head out. He headed to his apartments in the castle. Nestled in his private quarters, Alex had had a state-of-the-art kitchen installed for his eighteenth birthday.

He opened his fridge. There were no leftovers inside the chilled box. Alex didn't believe in leftovers. He made just enough food for himself. He never cooked for anyone. Aside from Jan. But he had assisted her in her vision, not his own

He pulled out the ingredients for a chocolate cake. He made sure to put in a pinch of cayenne. While he waited for the cake to bake, he pulled out a notebook.

It was the plans for a restaurant. There were schematics for the kitchen and seating area along with a menu of fusion foods from his travels far and away. It was just a dream, but one he liked to indulge in from time to time.

He'd spoken the dream aloud exactly once. But the girl he'd told his vision to had frowned at him, and Alex had dropped the subject immediately. He planned never to speak of it again. But there he was looking at the plans and thinking of her.

The oven timer went off, and Alex pulled out the tray. Ever impatient, he sliced into the dish before letting it cool. He did take heed to blow on the morsel on his fork before plopping it into his mouth.

And, it was perfect. Sweet and spicy with a kick. The

kick landed in his gut and urged him into motion. It asked what if?

What if he did put this plan into motion? What if he did open up this restaurant? What if he did live out his dream?

It was the sight of this morning's paper that cooled the fervor and left a bitter taste in his mouth. The morning headlines read *N'heir Do Well: The Cost of Prince Alex's Wayward Ways.*

It was an exposé detailing what the cost of his travels and gallivanting were costing the citizens of Cordoba. It was all lies. People wrote what they wanted to believe about him. There were times Alex believed it himself. Most of Alex's trips were comped by the ones who invited him. They earned more from him showing his face than the cost of his lodgings and food, and Alex was only ever there for the food.

Aside from his travels, Alex spent little to no money of the allowance allotted him. He didn't have expensive tastes unless it came to food. The restaurant was the biggest expense he would ever incur, and he was not about to put that bill on taxpayers.

He took another bite of the cake. The sweetness stuck to the roof of his mouth, but the spice hit him again in the gut. What if?

He looked down at his plans again. What if he did open his restaurant? He'd be the restless heir no more. The tabloids would have to find another story to write about him, and they likely would. But he wouldn't care because he'd spend the day in a real kitchen. He'd craft menus to take his diners' taste buds on the journeys he'd traveled. He'd open up a world of culinary adventure all while seated at a table.

What if?

CHAPTER TWO

As easy as pie was a misnomer. Jan Peppers knew that from a young age. Pie making was an exact and precise art.

She kept all ingredients, including the flour, in the freezer. Keeping the different ingredients as cold as possible was her number one rule. The colder, the better.

The fruit was cold. The water she leveled off in the measuring cup was ice cold. The butter was cold. Fat worked best in cold.

Jan shivered in the walk-in freezer at the back of her kitchen. Her slim body had hardly any ounces of fat beneath her pale skin. No matter how much she ate, she couldn't seem to keep any of the calories on her trim frame. The fat just never stuck by her. Probably because she treated it so well in the kitchen and preferred to bake with as much of it being present as possible instead of substituting it out for insane imitations like coconut, or avocado, or applesauce.

The thought of the fruit substitute made her shiver. Jan balanced the ingredients in two arms. She kicked the door closed behind her and began her assembly.

That fact that fat liked to hang around her but not on her had won her few female friends in high school and college. Her fellow bakers often cast her a side eye. No one trusted skinny cooks, especially a dough-slinging pastry chef. Even her customers were wary. Until they sat at a table with her and had their first forkful of what she pulled out of the oven.

The vents over the range filled the oven with the honeyed smell of heated fruits, the earthy smell of savory spices, and the warm, lusty smell of freshly baked dough. Jan pulled the golden brown concoction out of the oven just as the bell over her shop door dinged. The shop was already filled with her regular lunch hour customers. They'd all paused the moment the fresh pie came out of the oven, and its lush scent filled the small shop.

The pie shop opened at seven for breakfast pies. There was only one slice of Jan's famous maple bacon breakfast pie left, and Mr. Fitz was eying that from the far end of the counter as he finished his second slice. Today's special was a Tourte Milanese with layers of ham, Swiss cheese, and bell pepper. Only Jan had put a spin on the Italian dish and added a nod to Japan with yuzu citrus. The lemony fruit made a few of her customers pucker and then grin with surprised delight.

"Good afternoon, Chef Peppers," said Mr. Dalton, a regular who'd been coming to the shop since it opened three years ago.

"Hey, Mr. Dalton. Your usual?"

"You know me." He grinned, taking his usual seat, at his usual table, and going through his usual machinations of unfolding his napkin and wiping off the fork and knife she sat before him.

Mr. Dalton's usual was a regular old shepherd's pie. Made traditionally with potatoes instead of the daikon Jan had introduced two years ago. Infused with yellow onions and never again the sweet cipollinis she'd tried to sneak in last year. And always with the beef and not the bison she'd tried to spruce it up with last month.

"I'll just have a regular shepherd's pie." Mr. Dalton smiled up at her after he'd scrubbed the already clean silverware.

Jan tried and failed to hide her annoyance. She would never win a poker game. Her emotions were always clear as day on her face, just like the ingredients were always on her sleeve. It was another way she didn't quite fit into the culinary world. Her workspaces often looked as though a hurricane touched down.

"Sure thing, Mr. Dalton."

Jan sliced another piece of the shepherd's pie. It was nearly gone. It was a favorite of her customers.

Though the majority of her menu was an explosion of fusion pies, her bread and butter were the mainstays. Apple pie. Shepherd's pie. Pecan pie.

Most of her customers rarely tried her specials. They were mainly a tourist draw. But tourists came and went every day, taking their sense of adventure with them and leaving Jan stuck with the everyday common folk.

It wasn't that anyone said her creations tasted bad. They all just wanted the familiar. The tried and true. But Jan wanted to try new things.

She placed today's special, a chocolate pie spiced with cayenne, on its plate for the dinner crowd. She hoped it would get some love at the bottom of a few tourists' bellies. The pie would only keep for a couple of days, and she knew her regulars were unlikely to take on the dessert with its kick.

Jan sliced a healthy heaping of the potato pie for Mr. Dalton and brought it over to his table. The man rubbed his hands together and licked his lips before digging in. Watching him devour her food, Jan warmed.

It did matter to her that her customers were reluctant to take a risk. But at the end of the day, all that mattered was that her food sold. She just wished she could sell more of it.

"You'll be headed back over to the king's land soon with Ms. Pickett, won't you?" Mr. Fitz asked as she came back around the counter.

Jan nodded that she was. And she was looking forward to it. The people of Cordoba were much more open to fusion foods. She knew a certain prince who would certainly appreciate a Hot peppered chocolate pie.

"You'll be coming back though, right, Jan?" piped up Mr. Dalton. "You won't leave us for that fancy place?"

There was a part of her that wished she could. Jan was far from a restless soul. She craved stability and consistency, but only in her routines, not in her recipes. She'd long dreamed of traveling the world but had only left the country that one time a month ago.

She wasn't the type of girl that went on the adventure. She was the type of girl who read about it but not in a storybook or the newspaper. Jan read about other cultures and other worlds in cookbooks. She experienced those places in the fruits, sweet meats, and exotic spices from the safety and serenity of her kitchen.

She might be a tall, thin, plain girl. Such a plain Jane that even the E wouldn't stick to her name. But inside the kitchen with a mixing spoon in her hands, she could be anyone and anywhere she wanted to be.

There had been that one time that she'd been presented with a golden ticket to be that girl outside of her kitchen. Prince Alex had asked her to partner with him in a restaurant venture. He hadn't been serious. Alex had the attention span of a gnat and the commitment of a rabbit.

Even if he had been serious, Jan couldn't up and leave her responsibilities here. Unlike the Prince who was beholden to no one, Jan was trapped. At least she'd lucked out and gotten trapped in business instead of in marriage with her partner.

She'd purchased this pie shop with her former fiancé

a few months before their ill-fated wedding. In lieu of a honeymoon, they'd put a down payment on the business. Unfortunately, on the day of the wedding, he'd jilted her for his high school sweetheart.

Not only had her ex gotten married on their wedding day, at the ceremony their families had planned, and her father had paid for, but they'd also gone on an extravagant honeymoon in the Caribbean while Jan had been left to open up the pie shop the following Monday morning.

No, Jan just couldn't form another partnership with a man who didn't have both feet in the venture. Alex had likely forgotten about the rash proposal he'd whispered to her in an airport terminal as she watched her best friend get engaged.

Maybe in a couple of years, she'd have earned enough to buy her ex out of the business? Maybe when his ties were no longer around her, she could travel and taste the world's foods? Maybe she could open up another restaurant in a place where people were open to trying new things?

But that was a dream for another day.

The doorbell dinged, and the lunch rush began in earnest. With one last look at her fusion special, Jan pulled another shepherd's pie out of the warmer and began slicing into it.

CHAPTER THREE

*A*lex gripped the sharp object in his hands. He was surprised the shears weren't blunt. It was a wonder the powers that be trusted him, someone they constantly tried to manage and script, with the weapon. Didn't they all expect him to run?

Alex may run off to the corners of the world for days, weeks, and maybe one whole month, at a time. He might often find himself in compromising positions with some of the world's most beautiful and desirable women. But when he was needed, he didn't shirk his duties.

Luckily, he was entrusted with very few duties. Ribbon cutting was one of the few. It was a hard job to mess up.

He aimed the shears, tugged the two holds apart, and snipped.

The red ribbons fell away, and applause rose up as

though he were a child who'd just performed an elementary feat.

Alex looked up and put on his best, charming grin as cameras flashed and applause rose around him. Inside, he wished he could curse each of the people politely applauding him for a job well done. He wished he could show them what he could actually do with a sharp edge. He wanted to open his mouth and prove that he had something to say.

But he knew it was futile. They'd all already written the story of him. No one was interested in the truth.

"Over here, Prince Alex."

Alex grimaced at the sound of that familiar voice. He turned to find Lila Drake of the *Royal Times* newspaper. Esme called her the nemesis with the reports Lila had put out about Esme harvesting dragon eggs in the dungeons.

The story was preposterous, but tabloids didn't care about fact checking. Even though there was a kernel of truth after Esme took young noble youths on a dragon hunt a few weeks ago. It had all been fun until a stone dragon's head had rolled. The public ate the articles that followed up and had begun calling Esme the Dragon Slayer, and Alex's favorite, the Mother of Dragons.

"Prince Alex, what of the rumors of you and a certain French model spending time at a spa in Nairobi?"

"There's nothing to tell," said Alex.

"But there are pictures." Lila smiled as though she

had him cornered. "Ms. Bissett was seen leaving the same hotel you were staying at very early in the morning."

Alex had been in Nairobi. So had Chantal Bissett. The model had followed him there, but she only went so far as the luxury hotel in the capital city. When Alex had ventured off the beaten path of the Kenyan roads, Chantal had not followed. She'd flown back to Paris.

"I think something in the food disagreed with her," said Alex.

He'd been in the country to help install hydroponics in underprivileged areas of the capital and surrounding areas. The Kenyan population was urbanizing at an alarming rate. The vertical farms which required no soil or light were a solution to feeding the increasing population.

When Chantal had seen the fish in the water and learned that the aquatic life fertilized the salad on her plate, she'd raced to the bathroom and then out of the country. Suited Alex just fine. She hadn't been keen to eat anything but salad and turned her nose up at the national dishes.

"So you don't deny the relationship?" said Lila.

"You know I don't do relationships. I have no interest in being tied down." To emphasize his point, he rapidly opened and closed the shears he still held to make a slicing sound.

The men chuckled, likely memorizing the line to use later. The women tittered, likely setting their sights on being the one to change his mind. The cameras flashed, and the pencils scribbled, likely twisting his words into some new spin. He could just see tomorrow's headlines; *Prince of Shears: Alex the Great Leaves Model's Heart in Tatters.*

That was actually pretty good. He should give it to Lila for free. Instead, he handed the shears over and went into the restaurant whose opening he'd just lorded over. Eating there would be the perk of this particular day's duty.

"I am so pleased that you are here to share this moment with me."

Alex shook hands with the new restauranteur. He'd known the man for a few months having dined with him aboard a mutual friend's ship. The food had been good out at sea. Alex was excited to see what the man would bring to the shores of Cordoba.

Unfortunately, when the first course was laid before him, Alex couldn't hide his disappointment. It was the same fare he'd had aboard the ship. The exact same menu. The others gathered were delighted with their plates and dug in.

To be fair, the food was good. But Alex had had this experience already. He was itching for something new.

He carved the meat and found it perfectly cooked but under-seasoned. He dipped his perfectly crisp string beans in the glaze, but there was no kick. No fireworks went off in his mouth. There was no song on his tongue. For the second day in a row, Alex found nothing enticing or exciting about what was on his plate.

It was moments like these that made him itch to hop on a plane or boat and cast off in search of a new dish, a delectable morsel, a perfect bite.

Beside him, Alex heard someone sigh. It wasn't a sigh of pleasure. It was clearly one of disappointment.

Alex looked to his left. The other diner was older with silver hair. He had pale coloring which let Alex know he was not from the Mediterranean kingdom. The man was familiar, but Alex couldn't place him. The man caught Alex staring.

Instead of taking offense, the man put down his fork and offered his hand. "Good evening, your highness. I'm Gordon Rogers. Pleased to make your acquaintance."

"Gordon Rogers?" The bells went off in Alex's head, and he was able to place the man. "You were the restauranteur who discovered James Beard Award-Winning Chef Kyle Grimwalt. You also opened that restaurant in SoHo last year that earned Michelin star status in just nine months." The record was earning a star eight months after it opened.

"That's true," Mr. Rogers said, dabbing his napkin at his mouth and then setting it over his plate. "I'm an investor in this place, too."

"Congratulations," said Alex.

Rogers smiled, but it didn't reach his eyes. "Yes, I think it will do well. It will ... fit in."

"Yes," Alex agreed, looking around at the diners chatting over the food. None of them had their eyes closed as they enjoyed the food. Many of them had set their forks down, the food forgotten in favor of the company. "It will fit in with the other restaurants nicely."

It was not a good sign. In restaurants that earned stars and dishes earned rave reviews, the only sounds you could hear were the clinking of silverware against fine china. The murmur of conversation drowned out any sound on the dishware.

"The meat is perfectly tender." Rogers lifted his napkin as though to peek at the dish, perhaps to see if it had taken another moment to get itself together. "I just wish the spice had a kick."

"And the glaze, instead of sweetness I wish he'd have gone in a more savory direction to complement the beans."

"Exactly." Rogers leaned back, covering the dish again. He studied Alex as though he were a menu he was looking to order from. "I had heard you knew your way around a dish."

"Food is a hobby of mine." Alex shrugged. He hadn't put his fork down. Though the food wasn't a party in his mouth, Alex was hungry. He refused to let such fresh vegetables go to waste. He simply skirted the glaze. "If this royal gig doesn't work out, I'll open my own restaurant."

Rogers's brows rose as though Alex had told him his favorite dish was amongst the day's specials. "Why, that's a capital idea. Where would you open it? Here or in another major city?"

Alex paused in placing the food into his mouth. "I wasn't serious."

"Why not? I've heard your name mentioned by some of the finest chefs in the world. You clearly know your way around fine dining."

Now Alex lowered the fork. The crisp beans on the tines landed into the glaze with a plop. Alex was rarely at a loss for words, but Gordon Rogers had his tongue tied at the prospect of his dream restaurant. But there was still the matter of the crown's funds and the people's perspective of their philandering, freeloading prince.

"I would invest in it," Rogers was saying. "Not that you need my funds."

Alex scrambled to swallow the lump in his throat and seize this opportunity. "Contrary to popular opinion, I believe in partnerships. A blend of ideas."

"Do you have a chef in mind?"

"I do." His world was still spinning. The fireworks that had been missing from his mouth were going off in his mind. Was this really happening?

"I'd love to meet him."

"Her."

"Even better. Female chefs are the wave of the future."

"She is very special."

Rogers tilted his head and regarded Alex. "She must be very special indeed for you to want to partner with her in business. Business partnerships are harder to get out of than divorce. I have time tomorrow before I head back to the states."

"She's actually in the states."

"Perhaps we could set up a meeting sometime in the future?"

"I'm sure I can arrange something in the next few days."

Alex had proposed to Jan, likely the only time in his life he'd ever proposed to a woman. But she hadn't taken him seriously. He had a widely publicized reputation for non-commitment and impermanence. Hardly anyone in the world took him seriously.

But he was tired of roaming the world searching for the perfect bite. He'd had a perfect plate of food with her. And then she'd surprised him by spicing up the leftovers into something entirely new the next day. If this were truly going to happen, there was no one he wanted by his side but Jan.

He just needed to pack a bag, hop on his private jet, and convince a certain, precise, no-nonsense pie maker to take a leap of faith. Easy.

CHAPTER FOUR

Jan pulled the last of the apple pies from the back of her car. She wobbled in her red pumps as though the heels were the stem of the fruit. She spent most of her time in a kitchen full of hot pans and sharp knives. So heels were not a typical accessory to her wardrobe.

Except today.

Today she was out of the kitchen. Even if only for a brief few moments. Dear God, please let it only be for a brief few moments.

Her hair was done up in an artfully messy top knot that she hoped looked like it had taken her one thoughtless minute and not the hour it had actually taken her to arrange it. She prayed it looked as though her skin was naturally blemish free and glowing. She had on a pound of concealer on her cheeks to cover the blotches from being in a kitchen all day.

She took in a deep breath, but the body shaper she wore beneath her dress didn't allow her to get far. Jan was fairly flat chested with few curves. The shaper tried to push up what she didn't have and push in where her lines were straight. It was a great effect. The problem was that it came at the cost of her breath.

Jan looked good. She knew the food she'd made tasted good. She was determined to keep a good attitude through this ordeal. So, of course, when she exhaled, the heel of her shoe struck the curb wrong, and she went down on one knee.

"Whoa, I've got you."

The pie was liberated from her hands a second after her knee struck the pavement. Mud caked her shins and dirt filled her hands.

"Don't worry," said the man looking down at her, "the pie is fine."

"Oh. Great." Jan looked up at Chris, her ex. Of course, he'd saved the pie and not her. Typical.

She wished she could say that her ex was short and balding with a beer belly. Unfortunately, that was not the case. Chris was tall, tanned, and had a full head of hair. He was more of a cognac drinker than a beer drinker. The brandy was much kinder to the waist line. To be sure, Chris had to take into account that consideration.

Jan rose and brushed off her skirt, forgetting she had dirt on her hands which transferred to her skirt. She brushed the artfully crafted hair out of her face and then realized she'd left a smudge. She shouldn't have been worried. Chris paid her no heed. His focus was on the food.

"Oh, Jan," said a feminine voice. "You poor thing."

Inwardly, Jan groaned. Outwardly, she smiled up at Chris's wife. Marisol was the Barbie to Chris's Ken doll. The two were a picture. Both tall, tan, and gorgeous.

They'd been a pair in high school until Marisol went out of state, leaving Chris behind. Chris had turned to his old pal, Jan, and taken solace in her. Jan, the fool that she was, had mistaken solace for love. The moment Marisol came back to town Jan was left to console herself. Too bad the day Marisol came back was the same day as Jan and Chris's wedding.

"Chris, my hero, you saved the cake." Marisol looked to her husband with adoration in her eyes. Chris looked back with the same stars in his eyes. Jan rolled her gaze skyward.

"Oh, I'm fine," Jan said.

Chris blinked and looked over at Jan as though he'd forgotten she was there. Déjà vu. It was the same as their wedding day when Chris turned away from Jan in white and only had eyes for Marisol standing in the doorway of the church.

"Sorry, Jan."

Sorry, Jan. It was the same words he'd tossed over his shoulder at her when he'd run out the door with Marisol leaving Jan to face their family and friends.

"No worries," said Jan. "You saved the pie. If that's all, I'll be on my way—"

"You're not leaving," said Marisol. It was a question, but it sounded more to Jan like a threat.

"You can't miss my parents fiftieth anniversary," said Chris.

And that's how Jan found herself sandwiched in between her ex-fiancé and his wife heading into an anniversary party to the people who would've been her in-laws. Where was the ground when you needed it to swallow you whole?

Jan was only there to deliver the pie that Chris had ordered. She was obligated since she and Chris still shared ownership of the pie shop. She'd only wanted to drop the dessert off. She hadn't truly wanted to be seen, definitely not invited inside. The dress, shoes, and hair were only precautionary in case she was seen. But her armor had been dented, or rather, dirtied.

Jan had planned to go into the back of the house, into the kitchens. Not the front door. Not where everyone would see her.

She tried to backpedal, but that was twice as hard in heels. She teetered on the stem of her shoe, but Chris and Marisol propelled her forward through the screen door. All conversation stopped when she crossed the threshold.

Wine glasses paused on the way to mouths. Forks hesitated in lifting potato salad. Butter knives ceased their carving of bread.

Most mouths gaped. A few lips quirked. All eyes were on her.

It was like standing at the end of the aisle again while

the groom walked away with another woman. Chris and Marisol walked into the party presenting Jan's pie. Jan hung back, inches from the door. Before she could make her escape, her arm was grabbed.

"Jan, what a nice surprise." Chris's mom enveloped her in a warm mom hug. Then she pulled back, and Jan braced herself for it. "How are you doing, sweetheart?"

"I'm great." Jan may have put a little too much emphasis on the great. Her lips may have stretched too wide in their attempt at a healthy and adjusted smile.

"Good." Mrs. Hayes patted her hand as she squinted at Jan. The older woman dabbed at the smudge on Jan's cheek like she would've done were Jan still in grade school. "That's so good to hear. I worry about you, you know?"

A tick began in Jan's right eye as she tried to extract herself from her former, future mother-in-law. Mrs. Hayes's grip loosened. She turned away from Jan. All it would take would be one step back, a flick of her wrist, and she'd be out the door.

"Look, darling," said Mrs. Hayes. "It's Jan."

"Oh, Jan." Mr. Hayes swooped Jan up in a big bear hug.

The Hayeses were huggers. Something she had enjoyed as their future daughter-in-law. Something she cringed at now that she was the ex. The ex-neighbor. The ex-fiancée. The woman with the scarlet X on her dress.

No. Scratch that. The muddy X.

Mr. Hayes pulled away. Once again, Jan braced herself for it. "How are you, dear?"

"I'm ..." She'd already used great. What was another adjective to say that a woman wasn't pining over her ex, which Jan wasn't. Dating was the furthest thing from her mind. What was on her mind was tomorrow's menu. "I'm doing just fine, Mr. Hayes."

"Excellent to hear. I worry about you. I'm glad you're doing fine."

He said *fine* like it was code for something else.

"Your parents are just over here."

Of course, they were. Mr. Hayes steered Jan farther into the room. People looked away as she passed, but she could feel their eyes on her back. Her ears didn't have to strain hard to hear the whispers.

That's her.

Poor girl.

So desperate.

Jan was desperate. She was desperate to get out of here, to return to her shop where she was the mistress of her domain. Where she could pair things that at first glance shouldn't belong together, but under her expert hand, they blended into the perfect flavors.

"Jan? Bill, what is she doing here?" her mother asked her father.

"I don't know, Carol," said her father. "Let me ask the girl. Jan, is something wrong?"

Her left eye joined the twitch fest as she stood before her parents. "No, Mom, Dad. I'm fine."

Mr. Hayes deposited Jan in front of her parents and turned back to his other guests. Jan stood before her parents. Each wore twin expressions of worry as they looked down at her. The Peppers were not huggers.

"How's business?" her dad asked.

"It's going well." Jan placed her muddied knee behind her clean one and rubbed, hoping to get the spot out. Belatedly, she was sure she now had a smudge on the back of her left knee.

"Chris showed me the books," said her dad. "You two have a good steady income. That's the way to do it. Slow and steady. You'll have a nice little nest egg when you're ready to start a family."

"I'm so glad she and Chris decided to work things out," said her mother. "He's such a good boy."

Both her parents looked over Jan's shoulder at Chris who was in a corner with his wife gazing into each other's eyes. Jan's parents had adored Chris, thought he literally hung the moon. They were devastated when Chris walked away with another woman. But somehow managed to keep their seats when Chris returned to the church, just an hour after ditching their daughter, to marry his current wife.

On their dime.

"I gotta get back to work," Jan said, turning to head toward the back door of the Hayes's house.

She walked past downcast eyes, curious gazes, and a bit of finger pointing. She didn't bother to hold her head high. At her rate, she was likely to bump her crown on the chandelier.

She was nearly home free, being free of this particular home when someone else grabbed at her elbow.

"Jan," said Chris. "Let me walk you out. I wanted to talk to you about the business."

Jan held her sigh in as they walked to the back door. She and Chris had purchased the pie shop together. After his wedding, he'd agreed to be a silent partner. Yet here he was yapping away.

"I've been looking at the books," said Chris. "We're doing really well with shepherd's pie and apple pies and the mainstays. But you're spending too much on exotic spices. It's eating into our profits. Do you really need saffron?"

Yes, she needed saffron. She needed it for her lemon buttermilk pies. It was an essential ingredient. "Chris, I thought we agreed that I'll handle the menus, and you'll handle the books."

"True, but the books are telling me that we're wasting money on some things that are on the menu. You're a great chef, but sometimes you go a little out there with some of your pies. Like for United Nations Day. Who even celebrates that?"

For United Nations Day last month, Jan had made an assortment of national pies from around the world. There were one hundred and ninety-three countries in the UN, and many observed UN Day. Just not many

Americans. So many of the pies hadn't made it out the fridge.

"We lost a lot of money that week because of those exotic pies," Chris continued. "I want us to succeed. The more profit you make, the sooner you'll be able to buy me out. That's what you want, isn't it?"

It absolutely was. Then she could buy whatever kind of spices she wanted. Then she could make more fusion dishes and answer to no one about the cost of saffron or what she decided to put on her menu.

"I just want you to be happy, Jan."

Sure he did. Jan turned from her ex and headed back to her car. Once inside, she got a look at herself in the rear mirror and cringed. She'd been in front of all of them; Chris, his perfect wife, their parents, her old friends, all with a smudge of dirt on her face and mud on her skirt. Perfect.

She'd lied about getting back to work. She'd started closing up the shop early on Sundays to save a bit on money. The sun was setting by the time she got back to her little slice of the world. She'd moved into the apartment over the shop after the wedding that had excluded her. She hadn't wanted to be around any of the people from her past. She wanted to fixate solely on the future.

The problem was, the shop was having financial problems. She couldn't keep buying saffron to use in pies that no one but a few wanted to buy. At this rate, she'd be reduced to making pot pies in a food truck if she couldn't turn things around.

Jan pulled up behind the shop and put the car in park. She was ready to call it a day, but she wasn't ready to throw in the towel. Slamming the car door behind her, she fiddled with the keyring for the key to the shop's door. But once the jangling of the keys stopped, she heard movement in the gravel surrounding the back of the shop.

She had no weapon. What she did have was a kitchen full of blunt objects and sharp points. Jan turned the key in the lock. She reached inside the door and grabbed the first thing she could make out. A rolling pin.

She raised the pin. With all her might, she crashed the wood down on the intruder, hearing a satisfying crack like an egg's shell breaking. Her would-be assailant went down with a groan. Jan turned on the outside light and gasped.

"Alex?"

C H A P T E R   F I V E

*P*ain radiated from the crown of Alex's head. It was much like the pressure and pinch from wearing the crown jewels on his head. But, surprisingly, not worse.

Wearing the crown put pressure on his entire head. That particular misery went down his back as the type of ache that made legs restless. It weighed his arms causing him to want to free himself of the extra load and fly free. The crown had the added effect of blinding anyone in sight of it rendering them speechless. Or if they could speak, they'd blubber and stutter and spew abject nonsense to remain in its glaring light.

"Alex, are you crazy? What are you doing here?"

Alex blinked up at the blonde assailant that hovered over him. Jan smelled of warm bread and honey. Her hair was pulled back into its haphazard bun which she kept it in while she was cooking. But he noted a few artful braids and twists she'd never done before. There was a smudge at her cheek, but it was dark brown instead of the white of flour.

His gaze traveled farther down and noted the bodice of the dress she wore. It lifted her breasts and cinched her waist. Alex had only ever seen the pie maker in jeans and a T-shirt covered by an apron. He had no idea that beneath that fabric was a sweet, bountiful treat that would make a man's mouth water.

"What am I doing here?" He wet his lips. "Late night pie craving."

"That's not funny." Jan held up her weapon. "I could've seriously hurt you."

Alex winced at the sight of the rolling pin which had felled him. "Oh, I'm pretty sure you did."

"Probably gave you back a few brain cells."

She bent down and made a come hither motion with her hands. Her chest was right level with his gaze. That luscious bounty was only an inch from his mouth. Alex's stomach grumbled as though she'd presented him with a perfectly cooked, perfectly seasoned steak.

When her deft fingers ran through his hair, he yelped.

She frowned at him like a mother would a child with an owie. She made the come hither motion again. He knew now that he was meant to give her his head. The problem was he didn't want to bow his head and give her the back of it where the injury was. He wanted to tilt his head up and give her ...

He shook himself. This was Jan. She was not some

actress or model only interested in a photo opportunity. Since the day they'd met, Jan Peppers hadn't been blinded by the glare of his royal status. She'd squinted at the bright light his title afforded him. But in suspicion, not in awe.

"Why aren't you in your palace?" she said as she carefully ran her fingers over the bruise on his head. "Or on a paradise island sipping cocktails? Or lounging on a yacht eating canapés with sorority girls."

Alex jerked his head up and out of her grasp. His frown was filled with indignation. "Really, Chef Peppers? Sorority girls would never eat canapés. They'd be too worried about their bikini lines."

Jan crossed her arms and huffed at him. She was entirely immune to his charms. It was what he liked second best about her.

He saw a hint of a smile crack her serious expression. It had to be the canapés bikini joke. It was a rather good one, and only she would appreciate it.

She only ever smiled when he suggested they combine two spices together or mix herbs with edible flowers. Her eyes would light up when he showed her dishes he'd encountered from around the world. The few days they'd spent together a month ago, Alex had lived for those small glimpses into the real Jan. The Jan who was as fascinated and obsessed with foods as he was.

The other Jan, the business Jan, she kept herself closely guarded. Except when she was in the kitchen.

Over mixing bowls and cutting boards, Alex saw the real Jan Peppers. And he liked her immensely.

"I swear you're a menace," Jan said as she straightened, but her bark held no bite. "That still doesn't tell me what you're doing here, sneaking up behind me."

She stepped over him, and Alex realized she was wearing heels. He couldn't look away from her long, lean legs. He'd never seen Jan in heels. Just sensible, flat shoes. He'd never seen her calves either. Those, too, were on display. Along with a spot of dirt at her knees.

That slight imperfection broke his trance and made him smile. Jan was a tornado in the kitchen. By the time the dish came out of the oven, she was a ragged mess. The first bite of food whether sweet and savory, or salt and honey, or sage and hibiscus hit the tongue, the chaos in her wake was well worth it.

Alex rose and joined Jan in the shop, closing the door behind him. But not before peering into the shadows outside and shutting the blinds. "I snuck in because I was avoiding paparazzi. They're annoying in Cordoba. They're a hazard here in the US."

"So are single female bakers with a stock of dangerous utensils in their cupboards." Jan put the rolling pin on the counter.

"Duly noted." Alex rubbed at the back of his head. The lump was large enough that he'd notice it when he laid his head on his pillow tonight.

Jan's features softened. "I may have caused some real damage."

"It's not the first time a woman has tried to knock some sense into me."

"It's obviously worked all those dozens of other times."

Alex's mouth fell open in indignation. "Dozens? It's been hundreds, I'll have you know."

That elicited a laugh. Not a giggle. Jan Peppers did not giggle. She was far too serious. She did shove him in the shoulder. "Be serious. Let me have a look now that we're in the light."

Alex did. He took a seat on one of the bar stools and leaned his head forward. Jan ran her fingers through his hair again, and Alex closed his eyes.

The pain had subsided into a dull ache. With her fingers probing the sore spot a different pulse awakened inside him. He couldn't quite pinpoint the source of the throb. He was too busy concentrating on not looking down Jan's top.

Alex wasn't used to denying temptation. But he did allow his senses to open and take in her scent. He'd missed the scent of her, savory, spicy, and sweet all at the same time. Hopefully, he'd have Jan's aromatic bouquet around him on a more regular basis. He just needed to figure out how to make the right pitch to get her to join his business venture.

Alex opened his eyes and gazed up at her. More tendrils of her hair had escaped the clips. Her intelligent blue eyes were fixated on his head. Her fingers brushed at the sensitized skin at the crown of his head.

He was determined to have this woman.

In his kitchen.

Nowhere else.

She was the only one who could complete his vision.

"There's no blood," she said, taking a step back from him. "But you'll have a bump in the morning."

"Only one thing to do," he said, missing the smell of her when she stepped back. "You know the old adage; feed a bump. Starve a bruise."

Jan laughed again. It was a higher pitch, almost approaching a giggle. But not quite. "I'm pretty sure it's feed a fever, starve a cold."

"Starvation? That sounds like cruel and unusual punishment for the infirm."

"Fine, I'll feed you. I wouldn't want to be the cause of an international incident over your big head."

"My dear pie maker, so long as you put food in my belly, peace will reign through the ages."

CHAPTER SIX

"Ohhhhh, Jan," Alex groaned, his eyes heavily lidded. "It's the best I've ever had."

Jan hoped the neighbors couldn't hear the moans of pleasure coming out of Alex's mouth. Or the sound of him pounding his fists on the kitchen counter in her small apartment over the pie shop. Or the tapping of his foot to a rhythm that punctuated each moan and pound.

"Yes, yes, yes." Alex accented each exclamation with a jab of his fork.

He reached for the last piece of Tourte Milanese pie and slid it onto his plate. He was prepared for round three so soon after catching his breath from his second go. The man was an eating machine.

"Slow down there, tiger," said Jan. "And keep it down."

"Or what? I'll ruin your reputation as the best pie

maker in all the state." He took another bite and moaned. "Make that states, plural. Woman, you have a gift."

Jan couldn't hide the pride at his words. She felt a warmth spread through her, both culinary and feminine, at the sounds of his compliments.

Alex downed the last piece of pie, pulling the fork tines slowly from his mouth. Jan had to avert her gaze. But the sight was emblazoned in her mind. She knew what those lips felt like against hers. Alex had kissed her once before.

The kiss had meant nothing. It had been spontaneous, a congratulatory kiss after they'd won the Annual Cordovian Union Day Pie Making contest. He had likely forgotten about it. Probably had never thought twice about it. Jan wished she could say the same.

She couldn't. She still vividly remembered the press of his lower lip into her upper lip. The brush of his upper lip against her nose as he pulled away. The taste of his breath, cherries and black peppercorn, lingered for hours, days after. Probably because she kept making recipes with the two ingredients to keep the memory alive.

"That was a great start," Alex said. "Now what's for dinner?"

"You want more?"

Of course, he did. He'd been ravenous for her food since the day he'd walked into her pie shop and ordered a slice of each of the national pies she'd made for UN Day, and subsequently eaten them all. In Cordoba, he'd eaten his way through the high street showing her the country's exotic spices. Through all of that, he hadn't gained a single pound. Men.

"That only whet my appetite," he said. "I'm a man. I need meat. What do you have in here?"

He slid off his chair and reached for the handle of her small fridge. Everything seemed small in her apartment with Alex in there. The place was a study in efficiency. Her full bed took up most of the space. She'd brought up two bar stools to sit around the kitchen counter in lieu of a dining set.

She rarely had people over, so she didn't see the point. She spent most of her time downstairs in the kitchen. Her apartment was only meant for sleep. But now a prince squeezed his form around her and angled for her fridge.

Jan swatted at his hand. "Hey, you can't just go into a woman's fridge. It's private."

Alex lifted a single brow which would've been devastating if she was attracted to him. Which she wasn't. Despite herself, she liked Alex.

Only as a fellow foodie. He loved to try new foods. He had an adventurous palate. And he loved anything that came out of her oven.

But he was not relationship material. Just as his palate was open to trying anything new, so were his arms. She'd read the tabloids. She'd even seen him in action back in Cordoba. Women threw themselves at the Prince of Cordoba. Men walked away from a girl like Jan.

Jan understood Alex's draw. He was rich, handsome,

and oozing charm. He was also the type of man that had no incentive for settling down.

Not that Jan wanted to settle down. She'd tried it once. Being left at the altar had been enough for her to never put that much faith in a person again.

"Most women are dying to let me into their cupboards, Chef Peppers."

"Not this one, your royal highness."

He cringed. Jan had noted in their short time together that Alex hadn't preferred to be addressed formally. He had little interest in his royal duties unless they involved a meal.

"Personally," Jan continued, wanting to recapture the light mood of a moment ago, "I need at least an hour of prep time before I'm ready."

Alex let go of the handle and bent forward with laughter. When he straightened, there were tears in his eyes.

Jan wasn't sure where the quip had come from. She was a terrible flirt. But Alex had a knack for making everything a bit dirty.

When his laughter died down, he ignored her warning about her fridge and pulled the box open. Before she could stop him, he began pulling out ingredients.

"Sit," he commanded. "You made the appetizer. I'll make dinner."

Those were words Jan was not used to hearing. She sat back on her stool and watched as Alex cooked for her.

She knew he had some skills in the kitchen. He'd helped her prep for the pie making contest. Not just with the chopping and dicing. They'd come up with the winning recipe together. That win had been as much his as it had been hers.

What he pulled out of her small oven twenty minutes later smelled delightful. It tasted even better. Jan had the urge to moan and slam her own hand down on the counter.

"I'm stuffed." She threw down her fork, wishing she could unzip the back of her dress to give her belly the needed space.

"You have to admit it was a great pairing with the pie."

Alex had made pigs in a blanket with crescent rolls and a pack of Oscar Mayer wieners. Inside the rolls, he'd wrapped the wieners in ricotta cheese and sprinkled them with apple cider vinegar. On the side, he'd made a hash of carrots and potatoes seasoned with Old Bay crab mix.

Jan forgot her manners and licked the salty seasonings from her fingertips. Alex grinned at her machinations. He opened his mouth to speak, then closed it. He slung the dish rag from hand to hand as he took careful steps toward her.

"That's why we get on so well," he said as he leaned his elbows on the counter, bending his powerful body down so that it was level with her gaze. "We instinctively pair the right spices together."

She nodded at that. They did get on well in the

kitchen. If she'd found a man like Alex before her self-imposed exile from the land of relationships, she might have not left.

"Jan, have you thought more about my proposal?"

A kernel of salt went down the wrong pipe, and Jan coughed. Alex handed her a glass of water. She drank mightily before she was able to speak again.

"What proposal?"

"Back at the airport when Leo proposed to Esme. I asked you to open a restaurant with me."

She did remember that. Mainly because he'd leaned down and whispered in her ear. The smell of cherries and pepper had made her feel dizzy then, but she had her wits about her now. "I didn't think you were serious."

"I was. I am. What is it you say; only iron can sharpen iron."

"Yes, my dear prince, but you prefer your women to be plastic."

She'd meant it as a joke. The aim had been to put them back on their silly banter because surely that's where this particular conversation was leading. Only for the short duration of it, Alex had been dead serious. And now, his easy grin fell, like she'd actually hurt him.

He turned away from her, taking her unfinished puff pastry with him. He tossed the remaining half eaten blanketed wiener into the trash. Instead of addressing her, he turned on the faucet and began scrubbing at the plate.

Jan hopped off her stool and approached him like a wounded animal. He was a wounded animal. He was a man whose ego she'd bruised.

"Alex, you have an amazing palate. You're a really good cook. But …"

He turned and faced her. "But?"

"But you're a prince."

"Prince is a noun." He turned off the faucet and tossed the dish towel on the counter. "I want to verb. I want to do something with my life."

Alex reached for her hand. She gave it. Her hand felt warm in his.

"I know you think I'm a flake."

"I …" But she let the sentence trail off.

"I've only ever been loyal to food. I'm serious about this. I want to open a restaurant. And I can't see myself doing it with anyone but you."

It felt like a proposal. A proposal, and a walk down an aisle was the last thing Jan wanted to face again in her life. She pulled her hands away from Alex's and ducked them in the dirty dish water.

"People break their word all the time," she said. "I can't afford that."

"I've never broken my word to you."

"You've never had to give it."

"I'm offering it now."

"I don't want it," Jan snapped.

The tether holding all the pain of standing in the

aisle, the misery of others whispering behind her back, in front of her face, all the looks of pity weighed down on Jan, and she broke apart. Anger spilled out of Jan. Pure, red, hot anger. Unfortunately, it scalded the wrong man.

Alex had turned from her. He was putting his jacket on as he headed toward the stairs.

Jan shut her eyes. It took a few breaths before she carefully and meticulously retied the knot of her anger and disappointment and betrayal. Once the bow was pulled tight, she went after Alex.

"Alex, wait." She caught up with him as he placed his hand on the door knob. "I'm sorry. It's not you, it's me."

"I believe that's my line." He was smiling, but it didn't reach his eyes.

They stood at the door, staring at each other. Jan chewed at the inside of her lip, unsure what more to say. Alex peered down at her in the darkness, trying to see things she showed to no one.

"Is it my word you don't want?" he asked. "Or the business opportunity you don't want? Are you really content to stay here for the rest of your life making cherry pies? I know you. It's not what you're meant for."

"You don't know me. You don't know what I'm meant for."

"It's not a mediocre life with no spice."

She had no rebuttal to that. Prince Charming was offering her, an insignificant pastry chef, the opportunity to cook the way she wanted, in a new place, with a new flavor profile, for a clientele that liked the new and exotic. Why wasn't she even considering it as a possibility?

"I have an investor interested," he said. "That's how serious I am. Just let me bring him by tomorrow."

"An investor? But you're rich."

His grimace touched his eyes, and he winced. "I want to do this the right way. I don't want to rely on my family, my name, my connections, or those bank accounts. I want to do this as me, as Alex, not as the Prince of Cordoba."

There was so much earnestness in his eyes. Jan understood that. No one back home saw her as anything but Chris's ex. Poor Jan who was left at the altar. Poor Jan who wasn't someone's first choice. But Alex had said she was his only choice.

"Why me?" she asked.

"Though you're as brittle as plastic," he said, his grin returning, "we work well together. You get my vision. You're a beast with a baster. A rebel with a rolling pin."

Now she winced at the memory of nearly knocking him unconscious.

"Just meet with the investor tomorrow? I'll bring him by the shop for lunch."

Jan swallowed. She was unafraid to take a risk in the kitchen on a daily basis. It had been a long time since she'd taken one personally.

"What should I cook?"

Alex brought her into a hug. He squeezed her so tightly her nose mashed into his neck. And there it was again; the smell of cherries and peppercorn.

"I'm so happy I could kiss you," he said pulling away.

He gazed down at her as though he were about to. His sweet and spicy scent was clouding her judgment so much at the moment, Jan thought she would let him. It took a flash from outside the shop's window to jerk them apart.

CHAPTER SEVEN

"So, the plan I have is to start the flagship restaurant in Cordoba on the high street." Alex indicated in the digital presentation he'd had made for him before his flight across the Atlantic. "We'll get the wealthy elite on the inside of the establishment in the evenings. Since we're on the high street, we'll get a lot of tourist traffic. Later in the year, I'm very interested in launching a series of food trucks for more affordable fare for families, the working class, and the young adults."

Alex had had the best meals on the streets of Bangkok and Istanbul and, of course, New York City where they all currently were. Some of the most innovative chefs had no degrees. They measured by pinches and eyeballing, not cups and scales. Their kitchens were only as big as his bathtub in the palace.

He'd also dined at some of the most elite restaurants in the world where a single bite of food might set the diner back a commoner's weekly wages. Alex was living proof that the two worlds could exist in the same place and on the same palette.

"Cordoba has a history of blended cultures," he continued. "The menu and the flavor profile will reflect that."

"And the name?" asked Gordon Rogers. The man leaned forward, eyes shining with excitement.

Alex smiled sheepishly. Though he wasn't embarrassed. The smile was for effect. He may not want to use his family's fortune, but he was savvy enough to know he needed to leverage his family name.

"The Prince's Palate."

"How clever," said Phoebe Morgan. The real estate developer who only dealt with million dollar listings leaned back in the high-back chair and crossed legs covered in a bold red, high power suit. "I'm sure many women would line up to taste what has touched your lips."

She didn't have the decency to blush at her innuendo. Why would she? Power made not only men but also women heady with machismo. Alex had met her type many times before. Powerful women in leadership, those who had clawed their way to the top with no connections and had no qualms against putting their expensive heels in the chest of the next man. He'd had his fair share of the nouveau riche and long ago lost his taste for it.

"The slogan will be; Where diners can eat like royalty," Alex said.

"And will you cook as well?" asked Cody Walsh. The young man was barely past his quarter life but looked like he could easily pass for forty.

Alex had also known his fair share of tech millionaires who couldn't handle their newfound fortunes. Cody, with his blood-shot eyes and twitchy fingers, looked like he was on the verge of crashing and burning. From overwork, excessive play, or too much recreational substances? Alex would've put his money on all three.

"I know my way around a kitchen—" Alex began but was interrupted by Cody.

"I'm sure you do." The young man waggled his brows, but it came off looking as though his eyes were irritated.

"I'll have a hand in the daily menus," Alex said. He knew he'd be the face of the business, mostly. He was fine with that, so long as it was Jan in the kitchen, and he could discuss each day's meal with her. And maybe chop up a few veggies and toss in a couple of pinches of spice every once in a while.

"I hear you're quite the adventurer," Cody continued as though he hadn't heard Alex. "If you ever want to spice it up ..."

The young man handed Alex a card which read that he was a CEO followed by an unprofessional expletive.

Alex smiled and went to place the card in his pocket. At the last second his fingers slipped, and the card fell to the floor. Luckily no one saw it.

Alex was done with his wild days. He was a business

man now. Just like he'd promised Jan. The thought of her made him smile, just like the first bite into a newly baked loaf of bread straight from the oven.

"Speaking of spices," he turned the conversation away from his past and toward his future. "I've found an amazing chef. I'd love to bring you to her restaurant for a taste test. Lunch if you have no other plans. It's not far."

"A female chef?" said Cody. "How women's lib of you."

Phoebe grimaced at the younger man. "I'm free and famished. I'll get my coat."

"Hey, Alex, let me get a selfie with you to post on the Gram." Cody whipped out his phone, wrapped his arm around Alex's shoulder, and clicked off a few shots.

Gordon shot Alex an apologetic frown. Alex gritted his teeth and smiled for the camera. It was tough to do both. The unnecessary flash of the cell phone camera in broad daylight sent him back to last night.

He'd been able to shield Jan from the paparazzi. He'd shut her in to the shop and made his getaway. The paparazzi followed him back to the hotel, and he'd left them in the street. Of course, they'd been up and at it early that morning and had followed him here. It was par for the course. They'd get bored when they saw he wasn't sneaking off to see any actresses, socialites, or super models.

"I'm very excited about this," said Gordon once Cody let Alex go to send off his Instagram posts.

"I have to admit, I'm a little confused," said Alex. "I thought I'd get to work with you directly."

"All of my deals are done using investment groups. You want to spread your money around and not put all your eggs in one basket. It mitigates any potential loss."

"I'm sure that by the end of the year, you'll see a positive return on your investment."

"Oh, I believe you. This is a very low risk investment that's why I've only brought in two of my partners."

"I'm humbled that you have this much faith in me."

"Oh, it's not just the business idea, which I believe in. But if this does fail, and you can't return the investment, your inheritance will be collateral."

Alex froze. He had to swallow a couple of times before the words would rise to the surface. "My goal is to do this as my own venture and, apart from the name of the restaurant, keep the venture separate from the crown."

"I admire that. But I'm also a realist. You can't expect me to put all my eggs in the basket without any security."

Yes. Yes, Alex had actually thought that. How was he going to tell Rogers that he never had any intention of getting married, which was a necessary step in acquiring his inheritance?

"I assume this female chef, what was her name again? Jan Peppers, was it?"

Alex had never said Jan's name out loud. How did Rogers know?

Rogers tapped at the face of his cell phone. He pulled up a gossip blog. The picture showed Alex and Jan locked in an embrace. The hug had been innocent. Mostly. Though Alex couldn't admit that his body had warmed through holding Jan close. But theirs could only ever be a business relationship.

Alex didn't know the whole story, but he knew Jan's heart had been broken to bits and pieces. Unlike her Disney princess card carrying bestie, Jan was not a believer in fairytales and happily ever afters. It was probably another of the reasons they got along so well.

"My daughter showed me this before I left this morning," said Rogers. "I'm not usually one for gossip magazines, but she knew I was coming to see you. I assume this is the special chef you are partnering with?"

"Yes, that's Jan, but that picture ... it's ..." Alex's tongue tied. The picture was what?

It had been captured in a moment of pure joy when Jan had agreed to partner with him. He'd reveled in pulling her close. He'd said he could kiss her.

But he knew better. He knew Jan was the one woman he could never kiss, at least not again. Even more than proving his seriousness to this group of investors, he had to prove it most to Jan. If she walked, he'd be left with nothing.

"Or am I wrong?" asked Rogers. "Is she just an affair?"

"Jan isn't an affair. We're going to be partners for life."

They were. This restaurant would be open for generations. Alex believed that in his bones. He just had to make these other investors see that without the need for any collateral.

"Good." Rogers's eyes brightened with relief. "I'm truly happy for you both. You'll have the wife you want along with the inheritance and a restaurant all in the same year. Makes me even more excited to be a part of this venture."

Rogers stuck out his hand. Alex gulped, but his mouth was dry. The throb at the back of his head chose that moment to pound and cloud his judgment. Instead of setting the investor straight, Alex grasped the man's hand with his own clammy palm.

CHAPTER EIGHT

There was nothing like the smell of fruit on
fire. Or the sight of golden brown crust. Or
the heat from opening an oven door and getting a facial.

"What have you got there, Jan?"

Jan rose from the oven with her latest creation. The
pie looked like a sand castle. The top crust spiked up like
turrets. The pastry dough covering the sweet and savory
filling was a golden brown, much like an undisturbed
beach just waiting for its first footprint. Around the
center of the pie, sugar crystals sparkled as though
diamonds were buried in the sand of the dough.

"It's a chicken pot pie, but with rabbit meat instead of
chicken. And I also used quince, which is like a pear but
more acidic. There are chanterelle mushrooms, butternut
squash, and purple carrots."

Jan beamed as she held the masterpiece high in her
mitted hands. Her chest swelled with pride that the

ingredients in her mind had come together so well and so cohesively. She couldn't wait for Alex and the investors to arrive and try the dish. She should probably keep the specialty pie in the back so that other customers wouldn't see it and ask for a slice.

"Ah, that sounds nice," said Mr. Dalton. "Can I get a helping of shepherd's pie?"

Jan's shoulders slumped, and her smile pressed into a closed slash. She turned before she rolled her eyes, sitting the prized pièce de résistance on a platter. "Of course."

She couldn't get upset. There was one slice of shepherd's pie left on the dish, but she knew there was one more in the fridge. It was possible that she'd made her last shepherd's pie today.

She'd thought more about Alex's offer since last night. Perhaps it had been the flash from the photographer's camera that had done it, but a light bulb had gone off in her mind. Alex had essentially presented Jan with a dream job. Cook exciting new foods, her way, for customers who were interested in trying new things, all in an exotic locale. Where was the downside?

Sure, Alex had a short attention span. But they would have a business contract. Jan knew from experience those were harder to get out of than a marriage. Not that she ever had or ever would be married. But she knew her parents hadn't gotten any refunds from her doomed nuptials with Chris.

On the one hand, the business with Alex might fail. Most restaurants failed within five years.

On the other hand, she'd have five years of living her dream. How many people got to say that? The past three years had been a stifling nightmare living near and working with her ex. She hadn't received an ounce of support from her family or friends back home. But in Cordoba, she'd have Esme. And then there were all the new recipes she could try.

Jan served Mr. Dalton his pie with a renewed smile. She was starting to get truly excited about her future. And then the bell over the door dinged, and a cloud came in.

"I was supposed to pick up lunch for Marisol for a picnic in the park. But I'm running late. I'll just grab a pie from the display." Chris didn't even look up at her as he made his way around the counter.

Not only had Marisol stolen her wedding, reception, and honeymoon, now Jan was expected to cater their afternoon rendezvous? Enough was enough. But the crust nearly hit the fan when Chris reached for the special pie.

Jan placed her body at the pass through where Chris would have to exit to leave. He nearly bumped into her before he was forced to look up.

His gaze was a mixture of confusion, annoyance, and expectance. "I'm running late."

"That's not for you."

He opened his mouth as though to argue, and then he

squinted, peering at her face. "You look like you've had a busy day. Though it's not very full in here."

Jan's nostrils flared. Her chin went high, and she let out a loud breath. Before she could unleash, he set the pie down.

"How are you, Jan?" Chris reached out for her, placing both hands on her shoulders. His features rearranged themselves into a mask of concern. "I worry about you."

The tick started in Jan's right eye. She was so tired of hearing others say that about her. She was so tired of being looked at with pity. She was so tired of not being special enough for someone to choose her.

But someone had chosen her. Alex had flown across an ocean because he wanted Jan, and only Jan, to be his partner. Jan moved past Chris and placed a cover on the pie that would change her life. She reached in the display and brought out the very last shepherd's pie, put it in a box, and presented it to him.

"I wish you wouldn't worry about me," she said. "I'm perfectly fine. In fact, I'm happier than I've ever been in my entire life."

Chris nodded, his brows drawing closer, his mouth tightening into a thin, line. Clearly, he did not believe her.

"Actually, there was something I wanted to talk to you about. I have a new business venture."

"Not another weird pie, Jan. We want to make a profit here. I'm doing this for your future."

Little did he know, he would not be a part of her future. Jan wouldn't have to avert her gaze from any more looks of pity. She wouldn't need to plaster on a smile of faux cheer around people who were entertained by her misfortunes. Jan's future was bright and filled with weird pies filled with colorful fruits, pungent spices, and toothsome meats.

At that moment, her future came up to the door. Alex walked into the pie shop as though he owned the place, as though he owned the world. Jan wished she had that kind of swagger. Maybe, hanging around with him more, she soon would.

"You don't have to worry about my future," she said to her past. "In fact, you can have this business and do with it whatever you want. You can make boring shepherd's pies and uninspiring cream pies every day for all I care."

"Look, Jan. I'm sorry I hurt you on our wedding day. But I had to follow my heart."

"I get that. I'm about to follow mine now." She patted his shoulders and then gave him the cold shoulder. "Starting with this."

Jan picked up the pie just as Alex and his guests approached the counter. He was headed straight for her wearing the most dazzling smile on his face. For a moment, Jan forgot how to put one foot in front of the other, and she wobbled.

Alex caught the pie in one hand. Unlike Chris, Alex wrapped his other arm around Jan to steady her as well.

"Is this it?" Alex said by way of greeting. "It smells delicious. And you look delicious, my darling."

He bent down and kissed the side of her mouth, just

at the corner of her lips. Jan's knees melted into the consistency of pie filling at the impact of his lips.

It was the second time he'd kissed her. The first time had been careless. This kiss was calculated.

In the calculation, Jan knew it wasn't the full sum of what Alex could do. She knew she was only getting part of the equation. But even this small fraction of affection that he pressed to her lips gave her more value than any kiss she'd ever received.

"Please don't reach for another rolling pin," he whispered in her ear. "I promise, I'll explain."

He straightened and turned, still keeping her in the crook of his arm.

"Ms. Morgan, gentlemen, may I present Ms. Jan Peppers. The most talented chef I've ever met, and my future partner, in more ways than one."

Jan had no clue as to what Alex was up to. But just the look on Chris's face, the customers in the seats gawking with envy and not pity, it was all enough for Jan to go willingly with whatever Alex had planned.

CHAPTER NINE

*J*ust entering the pie shop heightened Alex's senses. First, the cooling scent of sweet basil tickled the tip of his nose. Followed by the earthy essence of cumin touching down on his top lip. That was met with the floral perfume of lemongrass on his bottom lip. And finally, the bitter balm of thyme cleared his palate and opened him up for more.

Alex stepped deeper into the shop wanting more. As he approached Jan, that sweet smell of cherries mixed with the crisp aroma of baked dough nearly knocked him over. The bouquet of scents swirled up his nose. They curled up on his tongue. They clung to his teeth. But the mix of heady smells had nothing on the chaste kiss he stole from the pie maker.

Alex rarely stole kisses. He was more often turning away from unwanted advances. Women frequently tried to plunge their tongues into his mouth and invade his palate. For the first time in a long time, Alex had the urge to invade Jan's mouth.

With just the slightest taste of Jan on his lower lip, he was eager to order up the main course. The amuse-bouche of the corner of her lips was a mix of salty sweetness and fiery herbs that threatened to drive him nuts. He wanted to slide his lips over hers, align their mouths, and plunge and investigate her palate.

Alex pulled himself a way. Jan was not on the menu. That kiss was a farce. It was a means to an end. One he had not yet cleared with her, and he wasn't sure if she'd be on board. He couldn't start his plea by pushing past a boundary he knew she didn't want him to breach.

He cleared his throat once, twice, and a third for good measure. "Jan, my darling, these are the investors interested in our new restaurant."

"Your new restaurant?"

Alex turned to look behind Jan. A lanky man in a suit too big for him gaped. His features were screwed up at the two of them as though someone had picked up the toy he'd just discarded.

"What's this?" the man demanded, surprisingly without stomping his foot. "Who are they? What's he talking about?"

Alex knew these questions were meant for Jan, but he supposed he should answer as Jan's wide gaze was still fixed on him. Likely trying to work out why he'd kissed her and was calling her endearments. He probably shouldn't have announced their plans so loudly while her current customers were enjoying their fare.

Alex turned from the disgruntled customer at the counter to face all the diners. "I'm sorry everyone, but it's true, I'll be stealing away your favorite pie maker."

There was a collective groan. Many people looked down at their half-finished pies as though Alex was preparing to take Jan's food directly off their plates.

"I'm not a customer."

Alex turned back to Mr. Lanky Suit behind him. He'd already forgotten the man was there. Alex looked at the packaged pie in the man's hands, then back up at him. Alex's raised eyebrows told the man that he begged to differ.

"I'm her current partner."

"Business partner," Jan corrected.

"Really?" Alex frowned. "She's never mentioned you."

"Well that's who I am," said Mr. Lanky Suit. "And she can't go into business with you when she's still tied to me."

Alex looked down at Jan. Her gaze was narrowed at the man in the suit. Alex was certain he didn't need to ask Jan if she wanted out of this particular knot or not. And then he recalled a chat with Esme. He remembered Esme telling him that Jan was in business with her ex.

Was this the same ex that had left her at the altar? And now he was trying to keep his hooks in her? Alex had never counted himself a hero. But at that moment, he itched for a cape.

"Well, consider yourself a free man." Alex pulled Jan more firmly into his side. "I'm buying you out."

Mr. Ex in a Suit balked. "Even if you could afford to, this business is not worth it."

"She's worth it."

Alex might not want to dip into the crown's funds for his own needs. But to save this particular damsel in distress from that villain in a cheap suit, he'd happily raise taxes. Being done with that conversation, Alex gave the man his back and motioned Jan over to where the investors had taken front row seats. Before they came to the table where the three people who truly would change their lives were seated, Alex chanced a glance down at Jan.

He expected to see anger on her face at his machinations. He was wrong. Jan gazed up at him, a bright smile on her face. It was the first he'd seen from her, and he was dazzled.

"You have no idea …" she began but didn't complete her sentence.

Alex wanted the idea. He wanted the scheme and sketches to the idea. Just to know what it took to make her that happy. Because he'd like to do it again and again.

"That was quite a show," said Ms. Morgan.

"Sorry about that," said Jan. "Some people don't know when it's time to move on." She was all grins as she watched her ex sulk out the door.

"Is this the pie?" asked Rogers, motioning to the dish Alex held in his hand.

Alex sat the pie on the table between the three investors. Jan brought over a knife and spatula and began the process of slicing and serving the pie. If Alex had not already known Jan was the one, just the smell of the pie would have convinced him. When he took a bite for himself, he was ready to give the woman anything she wanted.

The burst of flavors nearly knocked him to the floor. He looked over at her. Amazement and pride and excitement had to be clear on his face because he saw it reflected back in her gaze.

"This is delicious," said Gordon Rogers.

"Best thing I ever had," said Cody Walsh.

Phoebe Morgan said nothing. She was too busy chewing with her eyes closed and her head tilted back in what looked like ecstasy.

"You had me at the first bite," said Rogers. "I don't need a discussion. I'm in."

Cody gave a thumbs up as his mouth was still full.

"I want to say no because I'm sure you're going to ruin my figure," said Phoebe as she placed a second slice onto her plate. "But who needs a man when you can have pie like this."

"So, that's a yes?" Alex's heart pounded hard in his chest.

In response, all he got from the investors was a chorus of *mmmms*. It was good enough for him. He swept Jan up into a hug.

"We did it," he said pulling back from her. His face

was less than an inch from hers. If she truly had been his fiancée, it would've been nothing to lean in and kiss her. But because she hadn't yet agreed to that small detail, he decided he needed to carry her away from prying eyes.

"Please continue to eat up while I have a word with our pie maker," Alex said, pulling Jan into the back of the kitchen.

"We did it." She beamed once the door to the back closed behind him.

"We did." He nodded.

"And I'm free of Chris."

"You are," he agreed.

"You're not paying him off," she insisted. "I'll take on that debt."

"Not on your life. The check will be written and delivered to him tonight."

"Alex—"

Alex cut her off before she could begin to argue. Her ex was the least of their problems. "We have a more important situation that needs attention."

"What?" She looked at him expectantly.

"Those three want to invest, but they need collateral."

"I don't have much in terms of savings, but I'll contribute whatever I can."

The urge to kiss her again overwhelmed him. Jan was the type of woman who would give her last dime for something she believed in. "I have collateral."

"Great."

"I just don't want to resort to using it."

"I don't understand." She took a step back from him, getting nearer to the door. "I thought you were serious about this business."

"I am."

"You gave me your word."

"And you still have it. Just let me explain. There's this inheritance. It's quite a large sum. I'll get it on two conditions. When I turn twenty-five at the end of the year. And when I marry."

Jan's brows shot up. "You're getting married?"

"No." Alex raised his hands in a stop motion. "I have no desire to get married. But they know about the inheritance. If they think I will get married and will get the inheritance, they view it as collateral."

Jan nodded slowly. He could see the wheels turning in her head. "So, you're getting married."

Alex sighed. Why was this harder than he expected? Probably because they were the only two people in this room who didn't want to get married. "Not married. Engaged. By the time I'm twenty-five the business will be profitable and it won't matter. You see?"

"I see."

"You do," he sighed with relief.

"So, who's the lucky girl?"

"Well ... you, of course."

She stared. Her face crinkled in confusion. "Sorry." She shook her head. "I think your accent confused me. What's her name again? Wellou? Is that a common name in Cordoba?"

"Jan." Alex put his hands on both of her shoulders. She tilted her head back and looked up at him. "I'm talking about you. Will you be my fake fiancée for the rest of the year?"

"Me?"

"Yes, you."

Still, she stared as though she were trying to work out what he was saying. He knew his accent wasn't confusing. Jan just wasn't comprehending what he was saying.

"I believe in us, in our business," Alex continued when she remained mute. "We will be profitable. We won't have to go through with it. I'm willing to take the risk because I believe in us."

"I'd be engaged to you?"

"Yes."

"But we wouldn't go through with it in the end?"

"No. Of course not."

"Of course not."

She stared off at the exit door. Something crossed her features that Alex couldn't quite pinpoint. Regret? Longing? Resignation? But it was gone before he could pin it.

"Sure." She shrugged. "Why not? Wouldn't be the first time."

CHAPTER TEN

The last time Jan had packed for a trip to the kingdom of Cordoba, she'd had five hours to do it. This time, Alex hadn't given her much more time than that; a full day. This time she wasn't just packing for a long weekend. She was packing up her life.

Looking around the apartment over the pie shop, Jan was saddened to see there wasn't much to take with her. She'd already emptied her entire wardrobe into two suitcases. Being a pie maker didn't lend too many wardrobe changes. She mostly had jeans and T-shirts or cargo pants and cotton shirts. Her aprons were more plentiful than the number of dresses she had. All her shoes were practical; save the one pair of heels she'd purchased just to drop off a pie at her ex-fiancé's parents' anniversary party.

Never one for nostalgia, Jan hadn't saved her yearbooks. She didn't have photo albums. And thank goodness for that. She didn't want constant reminders of her past. But had she ever looked far into the future?

Most of the furniture had been there when she'd taken the place over from the previous tenant. All her time was spent in the kitchens down below. This was mostly a place to sleep. She knew for a fact that the palace guest rooms had nicer mattresses than the one she'd tossed and turned on for the last couple of years.

Other than the two suitcases of clothes, all that remained were her cookbooks. But she knew all of those recipes by heart. This new adventure wasn't about the past and tried recipes. No, this would be a brave, new culinary future.

Not to mention a new social adventure as well. She was engaged to a prince. In name only, not for real. But they'd need to keep up the farce in order to get the funding for the restaurant.

The scheme was something out of one of Esme's romance novels. Jan detested those kinds of books. They were entirely unrealistic, predictable, and impractical. Everything that she wasn't.

So why had she agreed to the farce?

The knock at her door jolted Jan out of her thoughts. Was it time to go already? No, she still had time left. But Alex was unpredictable.

At least he was knocking this time and not sneaking up on her. Jan opened the door and wished she had looked through the peephole first. Instead of seeing a prince with a glint in his eyes and a grin that Jan now knew the taste of, she was confronted by two displeased, gray-haired people on her stoop.

"Mom. Dad."

Her parents barged past and her into her home.

"Come on in." Jan shut the door with a quiet snick.

"What's this we hear about you running out on Chris?" her father demanded.

Jan looked over her right shoulder, then her left, but there was no one standing behind her. Her parents, the ones who had paid for someone else's daughter's wedding on their own daughter's wedding day were accusing her of running out on the man who was the cause of it? She had to have heard them wrong.

"Really, Bill," sighed her mother in her usual tone of disappointment. "Didn't we raise her better than that? Chris supported her in this crazy pie making scheme, and now she's leaving it all to him?"

How did he do it? How did Chris make everyone rally and flock around him even when his behavior was irredeemable?

"I knew we were right to be worried about her." Her mother took a tissue from her purse and dabbed at her eyes.

Jan's own eyes began their telltale tick. But almost instantly it stopped. It wasn't a tick. She blinked. The rapid opening and closing of her eyes washed something away inside her soul.

It was as though she'd been looking through a foggy

glass window. But now, with that one blink, the clouds had been wiped away. Jan saw the world crystal clear.

"She's just too modern," her mother was saying. Her mother had just turned fifty last year. "I know women these days can take care of themselves without a man." Her mother looked skyward as though she didn't know how that happened. "But how can she expect to do that without a job?"

"*She* has a new job," Jan spoke up for herself. "I'll be a chef in a new restaurant."

"What is this new restaurant?" asked her father.

"It's going to be called The Prince's Palate."

It was clever. It certainly would bring in more of a draw than Peppers' Pies. Jan had thought the name of her restaurant was clever, but no one knew who she was. The whole world knew who Prince Alex of Cordoba was. They'd likely be booked solid for months before the doors even opened.

"I've never heard of it," said her mother.

"Where is this place?" said her father.

"In Cordoba," Jan said.

"Where's that?" asked her father, looking to his wife.

"It's an island nation between France and Spain."

"I didn't know there was an island between France and Spain?" said her mother.

"It's where I was a couple of weeks ago. It's where Esme lives now. Remember, she's marrying the king."

"I've never heard of this place or any king but the one in England."

"Mom, there are other kings and queens and princes in the world outside of England."

"Sure there are. Make believe princesses in Disneyland and Disney World."

Why was Jan even arguing with them? They'd never believed in her, never supported any of her decisions other than the one to marry Chris. Jan's clear vision told her that one thing remained the same. It would be a waste of breath to try to explain this to her parents. Their view of her would never change, and there was nothing she could do about that.

"Listen, mom, dad, my business partner bought Chris out, for a very fair amount."

When she'd told Alex the value of her share, he'd doubled it without blinking. Jan had balked, but not loudly enough to stop him. Her freedom was worth the fat check Alex tore from his checkbook.

"Chris can choose to find someone new—he's good at that—and keep the shop open. Or he can sell the business and keep all the profits for himself. Either way, I'm leaving."

Her mother looked as though she were in the depths of despair. "Bill, talk some sense into your daughter."

Her father opened his mouth, but the doorbell rang. Jan was more than happy to interrupt the conversation that was going nowhere because she had places to be. She opened the door to reveal Alex who was grinning ear to ear.

"Hey," he said. "You ready to do this?"

She was. She just had to clear out the rest of the baggage from her home. "My parents are here."

Alex's grin fell flat. "I don't do well with parents."

He went to take a step back, but Jan grabbed a fistful of his shirt and dragged him inside. "Mom and Dad, I want you to meet Prince Alex of Cordoba. My business partner and fiancé."

Her parents blinked and then blinked again. Maybe the fog had cleared from their vision of her? Maybe they were finally seeing her clearly, for who she was, who she'd always been, and now the woman she was meant to be?

"Mr. and Mrs. Peppers, what an honor to meet you." Alex bowed.

A silly grin spread across her mother's face. "Truly? A real live prince? Our Jan?"

"Why, I never would have imagined it," said her father.

"Gee thanks, guys," Jan said under her breath. Nope. Her parents didn't see her anew. They still didn't believe in her.

"I certainly never imagined a creature like Jan could be real." Alex pulled her into his side and gazed lovingly down into her eyes. "Surely, you must've known from an early age that your daughter was the most extraordinary thing to walk this earth."

Jan forgot how to breathe. For someone who didn't do parents well, Alex was acing this particular interlude.

"If not as a child," he continued laying on the charm,

"then certainly the first time you tasted something she pulled out of the oven."

"Well," said her father, "she does make good pies. Although a little weird."

"No, they're not weird at all," Alex insisted. "She told you she won my country's pie making contest last month."

"You won a contest?" said her mother. "Jan why didn't you tell us?"

Jan remained mute. The twitch in her eye threatened to start. But even that nerve was too tired to be bothered. So, she simply closed her eyes.

Alex pulled her even closer until she was in the crook between his shoulder blade and his chin. He turned his head and planted a kiss on the top of her head. Jan felt the soft pressure of his lips at the crown of her head, and her stress melted away.

"I'm sorry for sweeping her away on such short notice," he said, sounding entirely unapologetic. "But there's much to plan. We'll be delighted when you come for a visit."

"For the wedding?" said her mother.

Jan felt Alex gulp. His Adam's apple worked against her temple. "Of course," he said. "But first for the restaurant we'll be opening together."

"A restaurant? What a brilliant idea," said her mother. "I've always said couples who work together stay together."

Jan could hear the hinges in her neck creaking as she

craned her head to gape at her mother. But her mother didn't see. Carol Peppers only had eyes for Alex.

"Oh, believe me," said Alex. "I intend this partnership to last a lifetime.

Jan knew he was referring to their business relationship and not the fake one. But something in her heart did a flip. She quickly told it to hush up. She would not be walking down any aisle that wasn't inside a kitchen. She would never make the same mistake twice.

CHAPTER ELEVEN

Alex snuck glances at Jan who sat beside him in the backseat of the hired car. She chewed her lip and thrummed her fingers on the door handle, right over the lock button. The door was currently secured as they maneuvered through New York traffic on their way to the airport. Every once in a while, Jan's index finger would tap the button, disengaging the lock, and setting the gears free.

He wondered if it was a subconscious move. Was she trying to get out of their deal? Was she trying to flee?

He had nearly run away from the scene with her parents. But he'd planted his feet and stayed. After she'd dragged him inside. He had to admit, he'd put on an impressive show.

Maybe it had been too impressive? He knew, that like him, Jan had no interest in marriage. That's what made her a perfect business partner. As well as a perfect fake fiancée. Their goals were entirely in alignment. At least he thought they were?

"I can send someone to pack up the rest of your things if you like," he said.

"Hmm?" Jan's thrumming stopped. When her fingers came to rest, they unlocked the door. She turned as though remembering he was in the car with her.

Alex had never been a second thought to any woman. He always had their full attention. Whether he wanted it or not.

He wanted Jan's attention.

"Oh, no," she said. "I have everything I need from there. If Chris wants to trash or donate the rest ..." She shrugged instead of finishing the sentence.

Her entire life was packed into two suitcases. If he thought about it, he could probably pack the things that mattered to him most in a couple of suitcases, too. Material things had never mattered much to him. Perhaps because he knew he could replace them. He had the money to buy whatever he wanted wherever he was.

Relationships, those he couldn't pack away. There was only a handful that he treasured. His brother and Pen, of course. Now Esme was added to his family circle. There were his friends, Zhi, the Duke of Mondego, and Carlisle, the soon to be Baron of Balansya. Other than that, there was no one Alex cared to carry around in his life.

He looked again to Jan and realized he could now count her in amongst that small circle.

Her fingers resumed their thrumming on the door

handle. Alex reached over and reengaged the lock. Before removing his hand, he captured her fingers in his palm and brought her hand into the cradle of both of his. For someone who worked with her hands on a daily basis, Jan's hands were surprisingly soft. She blinked up at him when he pressed his palm into hers and laced their fingers.

"How are you doing?" he asked.

Her gaze narrowed on him. Her right eye began to twitch as though there were something inside it.

"Whatever you're feeling, I want you to know that we're in this together." Alex gave Jan's hand a squeeze. "I couldn't ask for a better partner. I know it's going to be a huge success."

The twitch stopped as her gaze widened. Her lips parted, but she didn't say anything. Her gaze dipped to his mouth, and her pupils dilated. She swallowed, her throat working as though his words were hard to take in.

Alex knew it was difficult for Jan to trust men. She had to be after what he gathered her ex had done to her. Then he'd met her parents, who didn't seem to believe in her. All the people in her life were blind and had no taste. Alex was staking his life on this woman, and he didn't have a doubt in his mind that it would all turn out for the better.

A flash made him turn from her. Then there was another flash followed by another. He'd been so focused on Jan that he hadn't realized the car had stopped. They'd pulled up to the private airfield, and the press had found them.

Alex let go of Jan's hand. It was a knee jerk response. Anytime a woman was photographed with him, both their names got splashed across tabloids.

But it was inevitable with him and Jan. He'd already announced that she was his fiancée. It had only been to the three investors, her ex, and her parents. But that was a large enough group that someone would've contacted the media. Alex's money was on the pretend-player Cody Walsh.

He turned to Jan, re-lacing their fingers. "You ready for this?"

"Ready for what?"

He didn't have time to explain. "Just remember that you're in love with me and you adore me."

Jan made a sound of disbelief in the back of her throat.

"Okay," he acquiesced. "Just be quiet and look at me with puppy dog eyes."

"I'm a cat person."

He couldn't help but laugh. He liked this woman so well. "Don't worry. I'll take care of it. Just follow my lead."

The driver opened the door on Jan's side. Alex had wanted to hand her out himself, but he'd have to come around the other side of the car to do that. Unfortunately, Jan stepped out of the car on her own accord. They'd have to work on that.

The flashes blinded him as he rounded the car. The

calls of the reporters with their questions deadened his ears. He reached Jan's side to find that she stood frozen, catatonic before the cameras and the shouted questions.

His hand came to her back. She was as stiff as a board. He tried to urge her forward, but she would not budge. She only stared in abject horror at the crowd of press before her.

"Jan?" he whispered in her ear.

Her right eye was twitching again. He wondered if she were about to cry?

"Jan, my darling?"

She blinked, but her eyelid still twitched. She turned to him. Slowly, he saw the life coming back in her eyes. The twitch in her eye settled down.

Wherever she'd gone, she'd come back to him. Alex wrapped his arm around her and pulled her close. He had no idea what had just happened, but he was determined not to let her go.

"Prince Alex, is it true? Are you finally off the market?" It was Lila Drake.

Alex wasn't surprised that the rag paper had the funds to send their ace reporter on a continental journey. Stories about him were *The Royal Times*' bread and butter.

"Ms. Peppers." Lila turned her attention to Jan. "Tell us how a woman like you landed one of the world's most desirable bachelors?"

All mics pointed at Jan. But she remained mute. Alex

seethed at the comment, but he didn't lash out. He knew that would only play right into their hands.

He laughed to cover up the silence. "I never imagined in all my years that I'd find a woman such as Jan Peppers."

All cameras, microphones, and heads turned to him. Including Jan's.

"I've traveled the world for years. Have been to the most exotic places, met some of the most glamorous women. Meanwhile, the woman who would capture my heart was right here in the Big Apple."

Jan raised her eyebrows. Her lips parted as though she were going to say a quip, likely something about the only organ she had captured of his was his stomach. Alex took advantage of the moment to plant a brief kiss on her lips.

Partly to keep her quiet. Partly because, well, he'd been craving another taste of her since the other day. The scent of honey on warm bread met his bottom lip. But there was a hint of something more—there always was with this woman. Today there was also the spicy taste of ginger on her upper lip.

Alex had only meant the kiss to distract her. But he found himself sidetracked when the brief kiss lingered a second longer than he had planned for it to.

He couldn't help himself. There was something more on her upper lip. His culinary brain begged him to hold still, to take another swipe to figure out the component. But the flashes brought him back to reality. When he pulled away, he still wasn't entirely clear what the ingredients that made Jan uniquely Jan were.

Jan's eyes had stopped twitching. Her lips were still parted. Her body was warm in his arms.

"I fell deeply in love with her sweetness," he said. "She was the spice in my life I never realized I needed."

"How did you do it, Ms. Peppers?" Lila Drake looked skeptical. Her overly made-up face was contorted into a sneer of disbelief. "The women the world over will want to know. What's your secret?"

Jan swallowed. She gave her head a little shake as she turned to face the microphones. And then, in typical Jan fashion, she told the unblemished truth. "I just gave him some pie."

"Is that sexual innuendo?" Lila shoved the microphone directly under Jan's nose.

"No." Jan stepped back into Alex's side. "Just a secret recipe."

And with that, Alex gave Jan a tug. They ignored further questions and headed up the stairs into the awaiting private plane.

"That went well." Alex took his seat and strapped himself in. "I think they all bought it."

"You can't keep doing that." Jan stood over him peering down.

"Doing what?"

"Kissing me like that."

"It's part of the agreement. We're engaged."

"We're fake engaged. That means fake kisses. There's no need for tongue."

"I didn't ..." But he did. He had. "Sorry. Occupational hazard. Next time have garlic before I kiss you."

"But you like garlic."

Alex chuckled. He did like garlic. He'd never met a food or spice that he didn't like. It just so happened he liked the way Jan put them together, whether in a pie, or in a soup, or, apparently, in her own mouth.

"Jan? What happened back there?"

"What do you mean?"

"You froze when you got out of the car."

She took the seat across from him, fiddling with the safety straps before responding. Alex waited patiently. They had hours left sailing in the sky before they reached their destination.

"I just didn't expect there to be a crowd," she said finally. "Or for them all to be looking at me and stuff."

He knew that wasn't all. But she wasn't ready to tell him. They had time. They had a lifetime.

"Why don't we talk menus for the restaurant?" he asked.

And so, as Alex and Jan flew across the pond, they began to plan their future together.

CHAPTER TWELVE

"Best dish I ever had was in Oaxaca, Mexico."

"Mexico?" said Jan. Her brows shot to her hairline as she eyed Alex. They sat across from each other on the private plane. She was strapped in. He was sprawled back in his seat, arms stretched over the headrest, long legs outstretched just inches from hers.

"What's wrong with Mexico?"

"Nothing," she shrugged. "I just expected you to say some fancy, exclusive restaurant in France where you ate snails with truffle sauce."

"Oh, yeah." He rubbed at his chin, looking far off out the plane's window. "I've been to that place."

Despite herself, Jan laughed. When they'd first met, Jan had thought the Prince of Cordoba an entitled wastrel who lumbered from five-star restaurant to Michelin star restaurant. She was learning he wasn't that at all.

They'd spent the first hour of the flight talking about the menu of her dreams for their restaurant. There wasn't a single dish that Alex questioned or said was too expensive or too exotic. No, his eyes lit up and his mouth watered with each new ingredient she put forth.

The conversation easily morphed into their favorite dishes. She'd leaned forward, only to be held back by her safety belt when Alex began telling her about his culinary adventures in Kenya. His description of the dish known as ugali had titillated her senses. It was a simple dish of cornmeal and maize flour. But to hear Alex tell it, the mashed-potato-like dish would easily be favored at an American Thanksgiving served with a side of kale greens and fish straight from something called a hydroponic.

Jan had heard of hydroponic gardens before. In fact, she remembered reading an article about the technology helping poor areas in an African country. It might have been Kenya?

The urban gardens were all the rage in some urban areas in America. She'd been interested in installing one at the pie shop. But, of course, Chris had shot that idea down. She wondered if Alex might be open to it out in the back of their restaurant?

"I walked the markets of Oaxaca," Alex said as he leaned back in his seat. "Just walking the streets was a fiesta for my nose. I caught seafood with my own hands—"

"You caught your own food?"

He scrunched his nose up at her in mock affront. "Do you want to hear about the dishes or not?"

She did want to hear more about his culinary travels. These were the best stories she'd heard in weeks. Definitely better than her girls' nights watching romcoms with Esme. But still; Prince Alex? Getting his hands dirty?

Jan didn't relent on the skepticism inherent in her raised eyebrow.

"Fine," Alex sighed dramatically. "I was just off the beach. In a yacht. With a fishing pole cast over the side. But yes, I caught my own seafood."

That sounded more like it. Though she now had a vision of Alex without his shirt, flexing his muscles to haul a fish on the line. Jan gave herself a shake to get rid of the sight. It grew tenterhooks and clung to her mind's eye.

"When the local chefs cooked, they used recipes that had been handed down for thousands of years." He closed his eyes and groaned as though he were in ecstasy. "The moles, the chili, the chocolate, the chapulines."

"Ugh." Jan grasped her belly. "You ate grasshoppers?"

Though she feigned disgust, Jan had a fascination with people who dined on abnormal fare. Not that she would try any herself. It was horror stories for cuisine. The thrill came with the shock factor.

"They were sweet and crunchy," Alex insisted.

She covered her face and groaned. However, the smile on her lips made the sound come out as a half laugh. "What were you even doing in Mexico in the fall? I figured you'd be there for spring break. Was there a fashion show or something?"

Alex lifted one shoulder. He turned back to the window looking far off into the cloudless sky. "Nothing important."

Jan got the sense that whatever it was had been important. There had probably been a woman involved. Or two.

"You know, I remember reading an article in *Food Magazine*," she said, deciding to change the subject since she got the feeling Alex didn't want to spill, and she wasn't one for gossip. "There are some areas of Mexico where it's difficult for people to get farm fresh produce. So the government has begun a bus stop farmer's market program where the farmers bring their produce to the people. It's truly changing lives."

A small smile tugged at the corner of Alex's lips, but his gaze remained out the window. "Food can do that."

Something about that smile called to Jan. It urged her to probe, to dig deeper. It told her that there was a layer to this man that she had not yet witnessed. But just as soon as she leaned forward to poke at it, Alex turned to face her; his mischievous grin back in place.

"What about you?" he asked. "What's your most memorable food adventure?"

Nothing Jan had ever tasted had been as exotic as she supposed Alex's breakfast was. It had always been too expensive to eat out at the restaurants that truly piqued her palate. "My ex did take me to Le Fantaisie."

"I've been there. What did you have?"

Jan's smile was bitter. "The Troìs Fromage Gougères and the Pommes Duchesse."

Alex nodded and then nodded some more as though he were waiting for her to say something else. "That's it? Those are just appetizers."

"That's all Chris was willing to spend."

Alex tilted his head skyward. His lips moved, and Jan was certain she heard the word cheapskate uttered under his breath. "Well, did you at least enjoy the dishes?"

"I was expecting an out-of-body experience, you know, in my mouth. It was good, but I could've made it myself at home. It wasn't anything new. Food should transport you to the past or take you to some place you've never been. Just like when you described the chapulines, I was taken to Mexico. When you talked about the ugali, I was with you in Kenya."

Alex was watching her thoughtfully, his forefinger tapping his lower lip. "We'll go to France in a couple of weeks. We'll tour Montmartre where you can sample cheeses and pastries along the street."

"I can't just up and go to France."

"Why not?"

"As my boss, you know why not. I'm starting a new job, a whole new restaurant."

"This is a part of your job description, Chef Peppers."

It was a good thing the safety straps were holding her in place. Otherwise, Jan might have slid out of her seat.

"And I'm not your boss," he said. "I'm your partner."

With those words, her insides turned to mush like the dish he'd had in Kenya. She felt she was on his hook; like the fish he'd caught back in Mexico. She wanted to be reeled in. Getting caught by Alex, she had hooked into her dream.

Alex rested his head back against the seat and closed his eyes. A second later he was asleep. Jan was still reeling from what he'd just said. From what she had just done.

The reality of what she'd done was finally hitting her. She was on a plane over the Atlantic. She'd left her business, her family, everything she'd known to run off with a prince. It was the most outrageous thing she'd done in her carefully planned and measured life.

So why wasn't her heart racing with fear?

To be sure, her heart was racing. But there was no cold feeling down her spine. There was no bile on her tongue. The taste in her mouth was sweet. Her body felt warm. This had to be excitement.

She sat in the feeling. It wasn't a new experience for her. She felt it every time she heard the oven timer ding, and she pulled out a pie. But this excitement wasn't due to something she'd made. It was due to who she was about to become.

Jan figured she must've fallen asleep because when she came to consciousness, Alex was over top of her. He crowded her in, leaning over her seat. He smiled down at her with pure joy in his normally mischievous gaze. If he leaned down and kissed her now, she was sure she wouldn't mind.

"We're home," he said.

He unfastened her seat belt for her and helped her to stand. Her legs were wobbly from the long flight, and she leaned into Alex for support. He didn't seem to mind. He kept his hand at her low back as they stepped off the plane.

The moment their feet touched down on Cordovian soil, they were greeted with more flashes and shouted questions from the press. Some of the faces looked familiar. Had they all gotten on an earlier, faster flight?

"Smile," Alex said into her ear. "Pretend you like me."

Jan wrinkled her nose at him instead. He laughed and brushed his nose against hers in an Eskimo kiss. His lips he kept to himself.

The press ate up the show of affection. Cameras flashed. Pencils scribbled notes. More questions were shouted, asking for details about their love story. But Alex ignored them all and rushed Jan into a waiting town car.

Once they were inside the rear of the car, another blast of reality hit Jan. This time there was a tinge of worry that crept down her spine. "What are we going to tell Leo and Esme?"

"That we're dating."

"They'll see through it. They won't believe it."

"Leo will be thrilled. He likes you."

Maybe. More likely that Leo would be happy because Esme would be happy with this unexpected turn of events. Jan was sure her bestie would be the only one on board with the match.

"I still don't think anyone will believe you'd marry someone like me," she said.

"What?" He frowned. "You mean someone from New Jersey?"

Alex laughed, but Jan was serious. Their being together made no sense. She'd seen the women Alex had been associated with. Stick thin models who probably left the salad dressing on the side, and still didn't eat it. Glamorous actresses who commanded the entire room's attention when they walked in. She was neither of those.

"Jan, it makes perfect sense. Everyone knows my passion for food. Of course, I'd fall for a chef."

"Maybe Giada."

"An Italian chef?" he huffed. "I have standards."

But Jan was too worried to laugh at his jokes. In no time at all, they pulled up to the castle. It looked just as majestic as when Jan had left it a few weeks ago.

Would she be living here full time? Would she have to get her own place? She didn't even have any Cordovian currency.

Before her worry could escalate further, the door to the car was opened. Giles, the king's right-hand man who wore a permanent scowl, stood on the other side. He bowed to Alex and inclined his head to Jan as they stepped out.

"His majesty would like a word in his office, your highness," said Giles.

"Seems we have an audience with the king, my sweet," said Alex.

"No." Giles shook his head. "His majesty asked just for you. The future queen is in her rooms, Ms. Peppers, and has requested an audience."

Nerves wracked Jan's body as she determined how best to convince her best friend, the person who knew her best in the world, that she was in love and ready to marry a man whom she'd found insufferable just a few weeks ago. The doors to Esme's rooms opened, and Jan saw her friend. Esme stood in the middle of an opulent room. The former kindergarten teacher was dressed in a designer top, which likely cost more than Jan made in a year, and fitted slacks.

Esme looked placid and expectant at Jan as she walked into the room. Esme crossed her arms over her chest, and that's when Jan knew she was in trouble. Esme could still pull off the stern teacher expression. Jan was toast.

"That will be all," Esme said to the small gathering of ladies who'd been sitting in the chairs sprawled throughout the room.

The women, similarly clad in expensive, designer dresses and suits, rose to leave. But not before sneaking covert glances at Jan. Jan felt like a prized hog on display, just before it was thrown into the oven for roasting.

The doors to the room closed, and she and her best friend were alone. Jan searched for something to say in the silence. Once she had an opening line ready, she lifted her head and was nearly bowled over by the impact.

Esme rushed to Jan and threw her arms around her. When she pulled away, she was beaming. "You're going to be a princess!"

So much for convincing her friend about her fake love affair.

CHAPTER THIRTEEN

"What game are you playing at?"

Alex leaned back, but his brother's penetrating glare pinned him in his seat.

Leo stood behind his massive desk. It was a desk that had belonged to their father. Alex had been in this same position many a time in his youth. His father would tower over him as Alex hunched back in the seat, struggling to keep his spine erect in the face of the man who he seemed to continually disappoint.

There was never anything he could do right. Alex didn't sit tall enough. He never walked with long enough strides. He didn't speak with enough commas. He spent far too much time chewing his food. He went back for seconds.

The happiest moment in Alex's life was giving up trying to please his father. He remembered the moment with absolute clarity. They'd been in this very room. Alex had spent the weekend in the Bahamas sampling every variation of conch, a sea creature native to the Caribbean. While there, Alex had worked with an initiative that dealt with environmental pollution in the Caribbean Sea. But all the press picked up on was that he'd chatted up a Bahamian beauty queen who had also been involved with the initiative.

The paper with salacious headlines had laid flat on his father's desk. His father was red faced as he laid into Alex. He hadn't listened when Alex tried to tell him about the flavorful food. He turned a blind eye when Alex had spoken of the sea's pollution and his aide.

It was as if Alex was invisible unless he was making trouble or making headlines. The only one who believed the truth of his philanthropic ways when it came to food and feeding the hungry was Omar, the Marquis of Navarre. And that was only because he'd seen Alex working on his ventures a few times.

No one else in his family had cared or even considered investigating what Alex truly got up to when he was away. That day in his father's office, he had shrugged when his father finally stopped his shouting and demanded Alex shape up. There was nothing wrong with the shape of things. Everyone chose to see him in one way, so there was no harm if he kept doing what he wanted to do.

"Alex!"

Alex snapped back to the present and the current king.

"Are you even listening to me?" demanded Leo.

Leo's face wasn't red. He wasn't shouting at Alex. But he did have the same disapproving countenance to his features as their father.

"I don't know what game you're playing," Leo pointed a finger. "But if you hurt that girl ... Well, you'll have Esme to deal with."

That was a cringeworthy thought. Esme was a force of nature. Alex had yet to be on her bad side.

"Whatever scheme you've talked her into, you need to talk her out of it."

"It hasn't occurred to you that Jan may have fallen hopelessly in love with me?"

Leo snorted, finally taking a seat behind the big desk. "She's far too intelligent for such nonsense."

"Ouch." Alex placed his hand over his heart in mock offense. But in truth, Leo's words had hurt.

Leo had never pressured Alex to get married, not after his own arranged marriage. But Alex knew his brother expected him to settle down one day and continue the family line. Alex also figured Leo would be pleased that he hadn't brought home a socialite, or a model, or heaven forbid, an actress. He'd brought his own intended's BFF home. So, where was the praise and the cigars?

"She's not your type," Leo said. "You two have nothing in common."

"We have a lot in common, like our love of food."

"Similar taste buds do not a lifelong partnership make."

"Food is the common language of all human beings."

"I thought it was math."

"You would."

Where did Leo get off immediately dismissing that there could be anything between Alex and Jan? Why was it laughable that she could love him? Come to think of it, Jan had laughed when he'd first proposed.

"Is this some kind of stunt?" asked Leo.

"Jan agreed to be my partner in life."

"For life?"

Alex nodded his head. The movement was smooth, certain.

"I doubt it."

Alex pressed his lips together and blew a huff out of his nose.

"Is this a business deal?"

Alex chewed at the inside of his lip.

"That's it, isn't it? You two are opening a restaurant together."

Alex vaulted from his seat. His toes tingled when they hit the floor as though his extremities had lost feeling. His fingertips felt the same.

"But why?" Leo continued as though he hadn't noticed his brother's agitation. Leo had always been one for puzzles. "Why a fake engagement? Unless ..."

Alex paced the length of the room in an effort to wake up his feet. He scrubbed his hands through his hair and over his face to return heat. All the while he avoided his brother's penetrating gaze.

"Tell me you wouldn't. You wouldn't do this to get your inheritance."

Fire shot through Alex restoring feeling down to his toenails. "I've told you before, I don't want the inheritance."

"Forgive me if your current actions contradict you. Does she know?"

"Of course, she knows." Alex slumped back down into the chair. He let his posture go. He let his shoulders cave. "You think I would mislead her?"

By the look on his face, Leo did think that of him.

"We're not going through with it, the marriage. I have investors. The inheritance is collateral. But the restaurant will be successful by then, and I won't need to use it. I plan to never use it. I'll earn my own money in my own right."

Leo leaned forward, his brows squished together in confusion. "But why the farce? Why not ask me for the money?"

"Hmmm, let me think on that? I can't imagine why I wouldn't have come to you. You clearly have so much faith in me and my judgment and my abilities."

"Alex ..."

"Food is the only thing I've ever been passionate about in my life. It may be unbecoming as a royal, but all I've ever been praised for is my bad behavior. Behavior that's all staged and fabricated. Did you know that a few months ago, when I was in LA, it wasn't for the Oscars? I was setting up a food co-op in southern California where the underprivileged have no access to fresh produce.”

“No, I didn't know that. You didn't tell me.”

“I didn't think you'd care. No one seems to care. I got tired of telling the truth years ago because everyone preferred the lie.”

Leo pursed his lips, contrition clear on his brow. Then those same brows furrowed, and he tilted his head. “But you did go to the Oscars.”

Alex threw up his hands. “Of course, I went to the Oscars. I'm not a hermit.”

Leo's features relaxed, and he chuckled. With the sting gone, a light bit of laughter escaped Alex's chest as well. Leo might not notice the truth, but Alex knew his brother hadn't believed the worst of him.

“Alex, I'm sorry. I'm sorry you didn't think you could come to me with this venture now, and what you've done in the past. But, please let me try to help.”

Alex shook his head. His mind was made up. The press often accused him of being selfish and self-centered. For the first time in his life, he was primarily concerned with his own interests, his own benefits. He wanted to do this himself.

“If you really want to help,” he said, “don't let the press in on the true nature of my engagement.”

“What about Jan?”

His heartbeat quickened at the mention of her name. His belly grumbled at the mere thought of her. “I would never hurt Jan. She's far too good with a rolling pin.”

"I mean her heart? Women take things like engagements and marriage, even when fake, seriously."

"I have no interest in marrying, and neither does she. Which is why she's a perfect partner for me. In business," Alex made sure to clarify. "Our business relationship will last a lifetime. She'll be my work wife."

CHAPTER FOURTEEN

"It's not real," said Jan. "We're faking it."

"Yeah, right." Esme was grinning so hard she reminded Jan of the cartoon Grinch's smile when he was plotting how to steal Christmas from the Whovillians. Or, better yet, the Cheshire Cat's faceless grin when he was about to make mischief for an unsuspecting Alice.

For the last half hour, Jan had been trying to convince Esme of the truth of the relationship between her and Alex. Unfortunately, her BFF wouldn't believe it. Really, it was worse. Esme, who'd been fixated on fairytales and myths her whole life, was weaving more to the plot than there was present.

"Essie, we're doing it so he can get investors for the restaurant we want to build together."

"Oh, my gosh." Esme's eyes practically rolled into the back of her head. She pressed her hands over her heart and sighed. "If that isn't the basis for a romantic comedy, I don't know what is."

Esme had long since OD'd on Disney princesses and John Hughes heroines at a young age. The effects had ruined her in adulthood. Now that she was marrying a king and living in a castle, she was a lost cause.

"This is not a romantic comedy," said Jan. "It's not a Hallmark movie. It's not even an after school special. It's business. In fact, the only show we should be on is *Shark Tank*."

Unfortunately, Esme didn't hear Jan's pitch. "Alex is rich. He doesn't need investors. And if he did, he could just ask Leo."

Actually, that made a lot of sense. Why hadn't Alex simply asked his brother for the money? Why go through this farce of an engagement?

"Well …" Jan tried to think back to the reasons Alex gave her. "He said he wants to do it all on his own. Without his family's money."

"So he chooses investors, who have the condition of his inheritance, which can only be accessed after he's married?"

"Well …"

"And he goes a step further to choose an unknown pie maker as his star chef?"

"Hey!" Jan tossed one of the ornate pillows at Esme. The thing landed with a thunk right in her chest. It served her friend right. "I'm a pretty good chef."

"No." Esme tossed the pillow aside. "You are an amazing chef."

"And I'm not entirely unknown. I won Cordoba's pie making competition last month."

"Which was well deserved. You crushed the competition."

Jan lost the thread of the argument with Esme agreeing with each of her statements.

"Do you realize that you're also the only woman Alex has ever brought home?" She held up two fingers. "Twice."

"In a domestic capacity as a chef."

"Now you're engaged." Esme held up her hands in mock protest. "For pretend."

The queen-to-be leaned forward, placing her elbows on her knees and her chin on her knuckles. The posture reminded Jan of Esme's former profession as a kindergarten teacher. This was exactly how she'd look at the kids in her care when they told a tall tale.

Jan opened her mouth. Then closed it. This conversation was hopeless. No matter how many facts she put forth, how much reason she detailed, Esme would always prefer a fairytale retelling over the hard, cold truth every day. So Jan changed tactics.

"How are things with you?" Jan asked.

Esme's chin dropped to her chest. Her hands dropped to her lap. She flopped back in her chair and sighed.

"There's so much to do. I have to choose ladies-in-waiting. Did you realize there's still such a thing in the modern age? That's who was in here before you came. I was interviewing grown women—"

"To what?" asked Jan. "Wait on you? Dress you?"

"No, they're more like personal assistants because being a queen is an actual business, not just a fairytale."

Jan bit her lip. She so wanted to tell Esme that she'd asked for this. Now her wild imagination would have to deal with the very real consequences of marrying royalty.

"They'll help with my correspondence and organizing events. There are so many charity events. Leo steers me toward the ones for education. There are countless, endless dinner parties, receptions, banquets. I swear, I've gained ten pounds in the last month."

Jan rolled her eyes. Her friend looked as fit and shapely as ever. She knew the king would have no complaints with his wife's looks.

"There're openings, closings, festivals, funerals. Meanwhile, all I want to do is curl up on Leo's lap and kiss him all day and night."

Jan opened her arms, and Esme came over. She climbed on her friend's lap and the two snuggled in for a long overdue hug. It was so good to see Esme again. Jan hadn't thought through the consequences of Esme living abroad. They'd talked every day, even Facetimed while watching a movie last weekend. But she'd missed the physical affection that only a best girlfriend could give.

"I'm bumbling my way through this, Jan." Esme sniffled into her neck. "I'm so glad you're here."

"I am too." Jan gave her friend the strongest squeeze she could manage.

Her own engagement might be fake, but her partnership with Alex was real. So was their friendship. Those people, Esme, Alex, Leo, and Penelope, had believed in her more than her own family. They were her family. Nothing fake about it.

"Jan, you're here." Princess Penelope burst in the door.

Jan almost didn't recognize the little royal. Every time Jan had seen Penelope the little girl had been in pastel dresses and white cardigans. There had never been a hair out of place on her head or a spot on her clothes.

Penelope wore jeans and a T-shirt now. The knees of her jeans had mud stains. Her hair was streaming down around her face. She looked like a normal six-year-old girl now, and she flew into Jan's arms, piling onto Esme so that the three were in a huge hugging pile.

"I'm so happy you're here," said Penelope. "I hear you're going to marry Uncle Alex?"

Jan didn't like lying to the little girl. She looked to Esme and found no help. Instead, Esme raised an expectant eyebrow.

"That will make you my aunt." Penelope beamed. "I'm going to have a new mother and a new aunt, and they're two of my favorite people in the world. I am such a lucky girl."

Jan's heart squeezed. It wouldn't let any of the words she'd used to dissuade Esme leave her mouth to assault

Penelope's ears. Instead, she changed the conversation again.

"I brought you something. It's a very complex recipe. It's British, so we'll have to do metric conversions."

That did the trick. Penelope's eyes lit up with delight. The three women headed out and down to the kitchens, and Jan was saved from any more explanations as they began the complex recipe.

CHAPTER FIFTEEN

The next morning Alex waited at the end of the grand staircase. Jan was late. It was unlike the pie maker who lived her life according to exact measurements and kitchen timers.

Alex's mind went to the worst possible scenario. What if she'd changed her mind? What if she'd backed out of their deal?

There were other chefs he could partner with. Celebrity chefs who would jump at the opportunity to work with him. But his body chilled at the idea, his tongue felt fuzzy at the thought.

Jan got his culinary vision. Not only that, she thrilled him with each new dish she whipped up. She had a command of spices unrivaled by any chef whose table he'd sat at—and he'd traveled the world over. Once Jan traveled and experienced new dishes and spices, she would be even more amazing in the kitchen.

Alex wanted to be the one to go with her on those adventures. He wanted to be the one sitting beside him as she moaned with delight after each bite. He wanted to know her thoughts on how she'd twist that dish and turn it into something new. But he could do none of that if she'd left him.

His hands itched to call the airports and ground all flights out of the country. That's how she'd escaped last time when Esme came to believe Leo was about to marry someone else. Jan had come to him with a handshake and a fare-thee-well two days before she was set to leave.

He'd been disappointed. There were so many entrées he wanted to introduce her to. So many more desserts he'd wanted her opinion on. But after they'd won the pie making contest, she'd taken the money and gone.

He hadn't seen her all night. She'd been sequestered away with Esme. Had Esme talked her out of it? Had the fairytale-totting queen-to-be told Jan to wait for her true love to get engaged to?

Alex didn't want to block the path of love for Jan. He knew that any true love headed in her direction would have to take stock in her culinary talents. Which would likely make the man a new chum in Alex's eyes.

No one believed in Jan's skills more than Alex. He was firmly in her camp.

Of course, that didn't mean he was her true love. He hadn't bought into the notion of one perfect woman for one perfect man. He rarely had the same meal twice.

Except when Jan made it.

Since he'd been a young boy, Alex had always turned his nose up at the idea of leftovers. He believed plates should be cleared of food. Each meal should be freshly made from scratch the next mealtime.

But with Jan's pies, no two ever came out exactly the same. She'd add something new each time, changing the dish slightly. Enough so that he couldn't wait to taste what came out of the oven next.

Alex left his mental reverie and looked up when he heard laughter from up high. And there she was.

Jan came down the stairs with Esme at her side. Relief rushed through him at the sight of her. Then warmth flooded him as he got a good look.

Jan looked—quite simply—stunning. Alex couldn't take his eyes off her. He could hardly keep his eyes on her as his gaze traveled down from her chest to her hips. He hadn't noticed her curves before. They were always hidden beneath an apron.

She wore a dress that stopped just above her knees. They journey down to her feet was a long, shapely trek. Before now, Jan's legs were always hidden beneath long pants. Her feet had always been in sensible flat shoes. Today her legs stretched on into tomorrow and were lifted up by heels.

A throat cleared and Alex looked up into his soon to be sister's smug grin. Alex straightened his spine and wiped his features clear of emotion. It was too late.

"Am I overdressed?" Jan asked, frowning down at him as she stepped down the last few stair steps.

Alex opened his mouth. Sounds came out but no intelligible words.

Jan looked to Esme. "Did he say underdressed?"

"You're perfect," he mumbled. Of course, she not only heard but also understood him that time.

A pretty flush spread across her rosy cheeks, and her gaze dipped. If a compliment did that to her every time, he'd have to give her more. For now, he held out his arm, and she took it.

"You kids don't stay out late," Esme called after them. "Who am I kidding, stay out as long as you like."

They walked the hall in silence. Alex was conscious of his strides, making sure they weren't too long and would outmatch hers. Jan's fingers tensed and released at his bicep, which Alex was subconsciously flexing.

Finally, they reached his car. He opened the door for Jan and deposited her in the passenger seat. He took long strides around to the driver's side to join her.

"Sorry that took so long," she said once they were on the road. "Esme insisted on the new dress."

"It was worth the wait."

Jan shook her head slowly, but he didn't miss the flush creeping once again across her cheeks. "You don't have to say things like that. No one's around."

"I mean it. I may be a lot of things, but a liar isn't one of them."

"An exaggerator, maybe? I know I'm not a model."

"Definitely not."

The light pink turned a deeper shade of red as she turned and glared.

"Now, don't murder me just yet. What I mean is, I've dated my fair share of models so I can speak with some authority. The stereotype about them is largely true. They're beautiful on the outside with no substance on the inside."

The red was fading from her cheeks, and the pink was starting to blossom again.

"You're like a pie," Alex continued. "Beautiful golden exterior. But prick it, and that's where all the good stuff is."

He was quite pleased with his analogy. He could tell that Jan was too. She'd turned away to hide her bashful grin, but he caught sight of it in the side view mirror.

"Did they teach you that charm at prince school?" she said.

"As a matter of fact, yes. Charming pretty pie makers was my thesis."

Alex made a right turn after leaving the castle gates. It was a nice enough day to have the top down, but he much preferred to have a conversation with Jan as they drove to their destination. So he kept the top up on the convertible.

"How'd it go with Esme?" he asked. "Did she believe you?"

"Nope." Jan gave a shake of her head. "She saw right through it."

"Leo, too."

"The press had a lot of questions. I don't think anyone believes us."

"Because you don't think a woman like you would marry a guy like me?"

Her brows furrowed as she turned and stared at him. "Those words are my exact thoughts. But the way you said them you're denigrating yourself and not me. So I'm confused."

"I just mean that you're a serious woman." Leo's words echoed in Alex's head. "You're far too intelligent for the likes of me."

"I hadn't noticed that you were intellectually deficient."

"To the contrary opinion, I'm not. But the consensus was that if I married at all, it would be to an equally air headed socialite or actress or model. Not a talented business woman."

"I'm a jilted pie maker from Jersey. I'm pretty sure I'm the one who's gotten the come-up."

Alex merged onto the high street. It was the middle of the work day. Not quite lunch. So the roads were fairly tame. They'd be at their destination in under five minutes at this rate. He decreased the car's speed to prolong the conversation. He wanted to ask Jan a touchy question.

"Speaking of the dead weight you left behind back in Jersey, mind telling me what happened with your ex?"

Jan stiffened in the seat next to him. Her legs went rigid as though she were pressing on the brake to stop the trajectory of the conversation. Or perhaps she was pressing on the gas to get away from him.

"I just think I should know as your current fiancé," he hedged.

After a long pause, she shrugged. "We're from the same neighborhood. Our parents all ran in the same social circles. It made sense that we would end up together, but he met a girl at summer camp one year and they were inseparable in high school. She left him after they graduated, and he came back home and settled for me."

Alex wanted to question that single word; settled. Jan was a prize. Her skill alone would make them a success. But he kept his mouth shut, knowing the story wasn't finished.

"When his true love came back, he dumped me on our wedding day and married her instead. At our actual wedding. My parents stayed and watched. Well, they'd paid for it, so I supposed they wanted to get their money's worth."

"You're joking?"

She turned to him, pointing at her serious face.

"I'll promise you this," he said, putting the car in park and turning to face her. "When it's time to break our engagement, you can do the honors. Embarrass me however you like. Take your worst revenge fantasy out on me."

"Really? You'd do that for me?"

"Of course. We're friends."

Alex had been on the receiving end of a few exes of his own. Women were crafty when they were spurned. He saw that look in Jan's eye now. But when she focused back on him, the devilish look melted away.

"I can't do any of that to you," she said, disappointment laced in her tone. "We'll still be business partners."

Part of Alex wondered what maniacal plan she'd dreamed up. The other part of him was truly scared. He decided to drop it. "Yes, we will, because this is going to be a success."

"I know it will."

"We're here."

Jan turned from him and looked out the window. Her gaze widened impossibly large. Her mouth hung open. The pink flush returned to her cheeks.

"It's beautiful."

"Yes," Alex whispered, his gaze still on her. "It is."

CHAPTER SIXTEEN

Jan's pie shop had been sandwiched between a pizza parlor and a Chinese food place. Neither were upscale. Just the typical neighborhood haunts that locals would run into for a quick bite or a fast dinner. They often stopped into her shop for a quick slice of dessert to accompany their fast fare.

The place Alex had parked in front of was right on the high street. In fact, the street dead-ended, and the building was at the end of that cul-de-sac. It was not affixed to any of the other buildings. It stood proud and tall as though it never needed to lean on anyone or anything.

The little Alex had spoken of the building he'd led her to believe it needed a lot of work. It was nicer than a luxury resort. It screamed five stars. It shouted Michelin stars.

"Oh, Alex. It's perfect. It's beyond perfect."

"I don't think you can get beyond perfect."

"Well, you just did."

She turned to find him gazing down at her. At her words, something flickered across his features. He scratched at the back of his head and kicked at a loose stone in the pavement.

Prince Alex wasn't good with praise. Jan had realized that back during the pie competition when she'd applauded his sous chef skills. He handled criticism with a laugh and a brush off his shoulders. But praise made him fidget.

"Can we go inside?" Jan asked.

"We can do whatever we want. The building is mine."

"I thought you had to wait for investors?"

Esme's words sounded in Jan's ears. Despite what he'd said about the inheritance, Alex was rich. Had this fake engagement all been a farce to get her here?

"I bought it from an old family friend. He gave me a good deal because he's opening up a nightclub across the street. He thought a high-end restaurant would complement his new club. In fact, there he is now."

The man getting out of the limo looked as though he were a sheikh walking out of the desert and into an oasis. His sand-kissed skin gleamed honey-gold in the sunlight. His dark hair rolled down to just above his shoulders like a wind-swept sand dune. But it was his eyes that caught Jan's breath.

They looked like they didn't belong to him. They were blue like the sea after a storm. Then he smiled, and Jan forgot the name of the man beside her.

"Hey!" Alex snapped his fingers in front of her face, bringing her back to reality. He glared at the man who approached him. "Turn the charm offensive off. She's here on business."

"A creature as enchanting as this?" The man rolled his R's like a purring tiger. "She was made for the screen."

"No, she belongs in a kitchen."

Two pairs of modern, twenty-first century, liberated eyes snapped to Alex. The prince held up his hands to Jan.

"You know what I mean," Alex said. "Omar, Marquis of Navarre, please allow me to present Chef Jan Peppers, my fiancée."

Omar had been in the process of kissing the back of Jan's hand. With the announcement of her relationship to Alex, he dropped her hand as though it were a hot potato. "Your what?"

"I'm his fiancée," said Jan.

The Marquis' mouth went slack as he stared between Jan and Alex. Just another in a long line of people who wouldn't believe the two of them were a pair. Jan put her arm through Alex's in a show of solidarity.

The Marquis' gaze focused on their linked arms. Then back up to her. A slow, cautious smile began at the corner of his mouth. "Chef?"

Jan nodded.

"I suppose you two met in California before the Oscars?" said Omar. "At the food co-op Alex set up in the inner city?"

"Food co-op?" Jan began.

"No, no," Alex interrupted. "Jan and I met after that."

"Oh?" said Omar. "In Nairobi with the hydroponic gardens you helped install? Or down in Mexico with the bus stop farmer's markets? Or have you been on some other philanthropic trip that you haven't told me about?"

Alex pinched the bridge of his nose and sighed. He rubbed at his temple. He looked entirely uncomfortable in his skin.

He was fidgeting again. He'd just been outed as a do-gooder benefactor and not a bad boy royal. He was Clark Kent unmasked.

"In any case, my dear, it's a pleasure to meet you." The Marquis took Jan's hand again, planting a chaste kiss on her knuckles. "Welcome to the family. I'm excited to get to know the woman who has finally tamed our wayward prince."

And with that, Omar crossed the street to the other large building, the nightclub she supposed he would be opening in tandem with their restaurant. Jan turned to Alex.

"Why didn't you tell me about the food co-op or the hydroponics or even the bus stop food market?"

"It wasn't an important part of the story."

"It's the most fascinating part of your stories," she insisted. "Except, of course, for the chapulines."

He threw his head back and laughed. All signs of fidgeting were gone, and he was his relaxed, confident self again.

"I've always wanted to do something like that," she said. "Something where I could give back to the community using food. I've always wanted to tackle school lunches. Show kids that healthy food can be tasty and fun. Teach them how to prepare tasty snacks that don't come out of a plastic bag."

"I think that would be brilliant in the school system here."

"Really? You think we could do that? Later, of course. After we get the restaurant open."

"You could do it now in the role of my fiancée."

Jan didn't like the idea of that; the idea of doing it herself. Alex had built them up as a team. She wanted to keep it that way. "Why not both of us?"

"It can be both of us. But you'll be the face of it. I told you, whenever I try to do good, it gets turned around. Best if I stay in the shadows."

"But no one will see the real you if you keep the real you in the dark."

He reached up and pushed a stray strand of hair behind her ear. "The people who matter will."

She wasn't sure how they came to be holding hands. She wasn't sure how they came to be standing toe to toe.

Just as she wanted to partner with him in the business, and stand next to him with the school lunch venture, she wanted Alex by her side for as long as she could keep him there.

"We should probably have a look inside," she said.

He nodded, but he made no motion to move forward. His gaze dipped to her lips. There was no one around, which meant there was no need to pretend kiss.

Still, he came closer. Looking to her lips and then her eyes, clearly asking permission.

She didn't shake her head no. She didn't nod her chin in a yes. She held still.

No. She was moving closer. In minute, barely perceptible increments just like him.

First, their knees knocked as they pressed into each other's. Her free hand found its way into his palm. The top of her shoulder brushed against his chest.

She tasted a whiff of his breath. He'd had chives for breakfast. The smell brought her mind out into a field of bulbous green onions; garlic, leeks, scallions. Those would work perfectly as the base of a sweet corn cheddar pie.

Jan gave herself a mental shake. She needed to stay present if Alex was going to kiss her. Then she realized, she really wanted to be kissed by him.

His lips were nearly on hers when a flash blinded them both. Instead of pulling away from her, Alex wrapped her up in his arms. He shielded her, pulling her face into his chest and turning to seek out the danger.

His chest was firm and soft at the same time. There was a clear definition beneath his cotton shirt. But also a space to rest that was comfortable. Jan wanted to nuzzle.

"They're gone now," he said. "They got what they wanted."

They? Her brain was slow to make out his words. The flash had obviously come from a camera. Not a tourist camera by the strength of that bulb. It had been the press.

Had Alex seen them coming? Had he staged that almost kiss?

"That picture of us here will be on blogs tonight and all Cordovian media outlets in the morning. I can just imagine the headlines; *Serving the Chef After Hours*. Or some such nonsense."

By the haggard look on his face, Jan revised her thoughts of Alex staging what had just happened between them. He didn't want the press' attention. Especially if all they cared to write about him was negativity and lies.

"I'm sorry, Jan. I didn't think about them dragging you and your reputation into this too."

"Clearly, I don't care what people say or think about me," she said. "You've met my ex and my parents."

Alex hadn't let her go. He pulled her closer but not into his chest. He tucked her under one shoulder like a brother would a sister. Whatever possible passion had existed just a moment ago, that flame had been extinguished by that photographer's flash.

"Let's go and check out our new restaurant."

They turned their backs on the street and walked into the establishment. Though Jan's excitement had died down somewhat. She was a fool. Here she was literally walking into her dream business, but she was fantasizing about a kiss from a prince.

CHAPTER SEVENTEEN

"Children need to fill their heads with academics as well as the arts. Music, movement, expression, all strengthen the brain." Esme spoke into the microphone though she didn't need the amplifying device. Her voice rang clear and loud across the crowd gathered out in front of the elementary school as she spoke on her first initiative; an early learning institute for children under the age of six.

Alex stood behind his soon to be sister-in-law. The soon to be part of that title seemed unnecessary. Esme had been a fast friend the first time they'd met. He looked at her like she was a sister before his brother came to his senses and realized Esme was the woman he wanted to share his throne with, raise his daughter with, and spend the rest of his life with.

"She's in her element," Jan whispered, beaming proudly at Esme's command of the crowd.

Jan stood beside Alex. They were both on the stage alongside Esme and Leo. But they had taken a step back and were off to the side so that Esme could shine.

Alex had always been content to stand in the back and watch Leo at work. Leo had not taken a step back from his intended bride. He stood looking down at her. His hand was possessively laid at Esme's lower spine. His eyes glowed with something beyond adoration.

Watching Leo as he watched the woman he loved, Alex felt a twist in his chest. There were the private glances Esme and Leo stole, the secret smiles they shared. Alex had never felt that with a woman. He'd never considered exploring the possibility of those emotions.

Alex's own fingers rested lightly at Jan's low back, but he had no claim on the strong woman standing beside him. He'd never wanted any claim on a woman. His fingers curled around Jan's hip, bringing her closer. He told himself it was so that he could whisper back to her.

"They were meant for each other," Alex said quietly in Jan's ear.

He didn't miss the smell of shampoo in her hair. It was the smell of toasted coconut. It wasn't enough that she surrounded herself with food all day and night, the woman even bathed in its essence.

"I'm happy for them," she said. "They prove that some people who you'd never expect on the same path, could not only meet but continue their journey in life together."

"Why Chef Peppers, that was almost poetic. Don't tell me you've turned into a romantic."

She snorted. A few heads turned to them in the audience. Followed by a few flashes of cameras.

Alex pulled Jan into his hold. He rested his chin atop her head. He told himself it was to protect her from the press' scrutiny. They stayed locked in the embrace for the duration of Esme's speech. When polite applause sounded, announcing the end of Esme's speech, Alex found himself reluctant to let Jan go to join in on the praise.

"Thank you all for coming," Leo said, stepping up to the podium while still not relinquishing his hold on his fiancée. "We have time for a few questions about the new early learning program."

Hands shot up. Leo pointed to one reporter. Alex sighed when he recognized the reporter as Lila Drake from *The Royal Times*. She turned away from Leo and Esme and promptly aimed her mic at Alex and Jan.

"Prince Alex, how did you propose to Ms. Peppers?"

Alex raised his head from Jan's. He didn't come forward to speak into the microphone. He didn't care if his voice carried to the tape or not. He also held back because he didn't want to encourage anymore questions other than this one.

"I proposed in her pie shop. It was over a slice of pie."

The laughter of the female citizens gathered would definitely be caught on tape. If the tape recorders and video cameras hadn't heard his response, it would certainly be repeated for the straining ears.

"This was last week?" Lila continued her line of questions.

"Yes." It was all she would get. Alex had no idea where she was going with this, but he knew he didn't want to play along.

"What about reports that you were in Nairobi just two weeks ago with Chantal Bissett?"

He felt Jan bristle in his arms. Looking down, he saw that she was frowning—no. Jan was glaring at the reporter. Before Alex could come up with a dismissive quip, Lila turned her toxic gaze on Jan.

"Sorry to be the bearer of bad news," Lila said with a smile. "He's known as the bad boy prince for a reason."

"Bad news?" said Jan, her voice ringing loud and clear without the need for a microphone to amplify her. "Why don't you try reporting actual facts?"

Lila's eyes lit up like a Vegas slot machine. The press loved when celebrities pushed back.

"Ms. Peppers," said the reporter, "do you truly believe the playboy prince has changed his ways?"

Jan took a step toward the edge of the stage. Alex reached for her, but she slipped out of his hold. The Jersey flare in her boiled over like a pot on a raring flame. Alex stood back in awe at the display.

"He was there," Jan said, her accent thick. "If you took a moment to talk to any of the locals there, they'd tell you the real story. If you, ace reporter, only took a moment to look at the pictures, you'll see he was installing hydroponics to help people grow clean and wholesome food."

The pencils, which had been scribbling furiously at Jan's outrage, stuttered. The camera shutters closed. Each face in the crowd frowned as though trying to comprehend the turn of events.

"Cordoba's playboy prince," Jan spat out the words that Alex had detested all his life, "has been more concerned with feeding the world's downtrodden population than he has cared to chase skinny twigs in a skirt. So, no, I don't think he's changed at all. You all have never seen who he truly is."

Silence reigned in the crowd. The revelation made everyone in attendance fidget. Not Alex. For the first time in his life, he was perfectly calm and content. He wanted the moment to go on forever.

"In just a few short weeks, I've come to know the prince better than many of his own countrymen. I can't even express how proud I am that he chose me to be his partner. I would never ask him to change a single thing. I like him as he is."

Jan looked at him, really looked at him. Under her gaze, Alex felt something shift inside. He didn't think he knew the words to express what was happening inside him.

"Well, maybe except the whole milk in tea business." Jan's features crumpled in distaste. "It's truly barbaric."

"It may be an acquired taste," he said.

"You can keep that particular taste to yourself."

"Noted, my sweet."

And then, because he could, Alex stole a kiss. It was just a light, little kiss. It was frowned upon for royals to show affection in public. But he was a rebel royal, and he was engaged to this spicy woman with a sweet tooth.

Jan gasped at the contact. Her eyes were dazed as he pulled away. He didn't let her get far. He pulled her close and walked her off the stage to the flash of cameras and the shouts of more questions.

They reached the waiting car. Alex handed Jan inside. Then Leo did the same with Esme. Before Alex could climb in, Leo put a hand to his shoulder.

"Fake, huh?" asked Leo.

Alex had no comment. He couldn't be bothered to form any words. He was far too busy swiping at his bottom lip, trying to take in more of Jan's sweet and spicy taste.

CHAPTER EIGHTEEN

"What about a dash of Sriracha?"

"That's insane." Jan stayed Alex's hand before he could sprinkle the spicy ingredient into her mix. "Sriracha and peanut butter?"

They were inside their soon to be renovated restaurant. The space only needed to be painted, decorated, and filled with tables and chairs. The kitchen was in remarkable shape. There was a large picturesque window that looked out at the Cordovian mountains in the distance. There was space for a deck if they ever wanted to serve food directly from the kitchen to customers on a patio bar.

Her old kitchen had no windows, and even if they did, she'd only see the dirty alleyway and trash bins. Jan couldn't wait to cook in this space and be greeted with that sight every day. But first, she had to save her dish from her partner's insanity.

Alex managed to toss the spicy sriracha in despite her protests. He gave it a stir and then scooped a bit out. He held the spoon out for her. His grin was wide, his brows raised in a challenge.

Jan crossed her arms over her shoulders. She pressed her lips firmly together. She was adventurous when it came to food, but there was no way that combination would work.

Alex airplaned the spoon toward her. "Open wide for some yum yum."

She shook her head like an infant. When he began to make engine noises, she couldn't help it. She burst out laughing. That's when he landed the food in her mouth. Flavor burst on Jan's tongue, and her eyes widened.

"Good?" he asked, swiping a dab at her cheek with his thumb.

"Delicious," she admitted.

His finger lingered on her cheek a moment too long. His gaze dipped to her lips. Jan licked at her bottom lip to gather more of the hot and nutty flavors.

Alex swallowed hard, his Adam's apple bobbing with the motion. He took his hand away and fidgeted. Was it from the compliment? Or their closeness? She wasn't sure?

"We make a good team," he said.

"Sugar and spice."

"I'm the sugar," he insisted.

She giggled. Then she covered her mouth. Jan Peppers never giggled. What had gotten into her?

Probably that light peck he'd given her earlier at Esme's speech. She'd known it was for show for the press, but the little kiss had had a big impact on her.

The whole show of affection he'd displayed before the kiss, holding her in his arms, resting his head atop her head like they were a real couple. It short circuited something in her brain. She was certain that was why she'd taken that reporter to task.

No. If she were honest, she'd have to admit that the two incidences were separate. When that reporter had begun intentionally misinterpreting or simply outright ignoring facts to paint Alex in a negative light, it had ticked off Jan.

Which was funny because Jan never stood up for herself. But cast someone she cared about in a negative light, and she turned into a pit bull. If she ever encountered that nasty reporter again, she'd be sure to develop a case of lockjaw.

Alex had just stood there and taken it. He'd told her that it was pointless to fight back. The press—and the people—had no intentions of recasting him in a more appropriate role. But they'd be fools to think that Jan would be cast as a clueless, pitiful bride to be.

Alex chopped up apples while she diced carrots for their creation. She watched as his hands handled both the blade and the fruit with deft fingers. She wondered what those hands would feel like cupping her cheek, pressing at her back.

The problem was, she knew exactly what they'd feel like. She'd felt them more than once over the past few days, and she was hungry for more.

If she were being honest, his every touch, his every word, his every glance was affecting her. She had to keep reminding herself that it wasn't real. None of it.

They were playing for the cameras so that they could make their dreams come true. Was she going to last months in this fake engagement? With only just a couple of days, it was feeling more and more real to her.

The oven timer dinged. She moved to place on her oven mitts. As she did so, she felt him move behind her. He didn't touch her. Still, she'd grown so aware of him she felt she knew where he was headed before he set in motion.

"I was thinking," he said coming to lean against the counter as she removed the pie from the oven's belly.

She sighed dramatically as she placed the hot dish on the stovetop. "Recipes change when you do that."

Alex chuckled lightly. He ran his hand over the back of his neck. He was fidgeting again. "I was thinking we could get away this weekend. Maybe sail over to Spain and—"

"Sail to Spain?"

"Yeah, there's a dish I want you to try at this tiny hole in the wall restaurant."

"You want to sail to Spain for dinner?" Jan removed her oven mitts and turned to face him.

He shrugged as though he'd asked her to come down to breakfast.

"For work, you mean?"

Again he shrugged, but his hand went again to the back of his neck. He rubbed the spot fiercely as he spoke, not quite meeting her gaze. "You're my fiancée. I don't need a reason to wine and dine you."

There was that fuzzy line again. Jan liked exact measurements and precise times. She needed things to be crystal clear. She picked up the apples he'd chopped and poured them into the mixing bowl with the sriracha and peanut butter.

"We can't run off to Spain," she said, picking up a mixing spoon. "There's so much to do here."

Alex took the mixing spoon from her. "You don't have to do it all. You'll have a full kitchen staff. And I'll be here every step of the way, adding a pinch of spice to each of the dishes."

She grinned at those words. Every time he said a variation of them—that he'd be there, that he was her partner, that she wasn't alone—her heart did a complicated somersault.

"You're going to be a princess," he said. "You deserve to be pampered."

"But ..." She tripped over her tongue and had to swallow before she could get the rest of the words out. The sweet and spicy taste of their combined mixture now tasted bitter. "But it's all fake. Us, I mean. We're just pretending."

"Just the part we want them to believe is fake. You and I ..."

Jan held her breath so she would not miss a single word, not a single shift of his facial expression.

"You and I are gonna be partners for life."

It wasn't a declaration of love. She wasn't even sure if it were a request for a date. She only knew she wanted to go. She wanted to go wherever this man wanted to take her. She wanted to eat whatever he put on her fork.

Unfortunately, before she could answer, a flash blared through the back window and into her eyes.

Alex pulled her to him, just like he'd done before. He used his body to shield her. Jan found herself once again in that soft space on his chest where she knew his heart lay beneath the fabric of his clothing and the warmth of his skin.

"It's the press again," he growled.

Jan looked up, but not out of the window. She fixed her gaze on Alex and his lips. "Let's give them what they want."

His gaze broke away from the window. His features softened when he looked down at her. He didn't ask for clarification on her words. He knew exactly what she meant.

She was already in his arms. Their bodies were so close that their heartbeats were beginning to sync. Alex brought his hand to her cheek.

Jan's lashes fluttered. She fought to keep her eyes open. She didn't want to miss a moment of this. Not the sight of his lips brushing lightly over hers. Not the soft bump of his nose against hers. Not the question in his eyes just as he pressed his lips a touch more firmly against hers, deepening the kiss.

It was heady. Fiery sriracha, earthy peanut butter, tangy apples, and Alex.

"Are they still there?" Alex asked nuzzling her ear.

It took Jan a moment to focus. When her vision cleared, the window was clear. The photographer was walking away, looking down at this camera in one hand and fist-pumping the air with the other.

"Um, yeah, he's still there."

"Okay." Alex left her ear, trailing kisses along the underside of her cheek until he made his way back to her mouth where he took a healthy sample of her lips.

Jan felt not a single twinge of remorse at her white lie. Technically, the cameraman was still there. But after another moment kissing Alex, Jan forgot all about the intruder.

ells rang in his ear. Cheap perfume and sweat clogged his nostrils. Alcohol burned his tongue. Those were all fine assaults on his senses. What Alex hadn't much cared for was the bare flesh gyrating over the plate the waiter had just sat down before him.

As soon as he'd seen the day's special on the menu, his mouth had started salivating. He'd had Marrakchia before when he'd visited Morocco. When he'd heard that the chef of this local Cordovian club had installed a tangia, a clay pot used to slow cook meat, Alex had called ahead to order the dish. The onion saturated lamb dish had been placed on his table just moments after he'd taken his seat. It was piping hot. The aromatic smoke of turmeric and ginger curled around his nose. Then whirling hips had interrupted his first bite.

"Do you mind?" he asked the dancer.

If she heard him over the din of pulsing beats, she made no indication. She rotated her hips even faster in a series of syncopated motions meant to entice thirsty men. Alex wasn't interested in the dancer's milkshake. He was hungry for the dish. He clutched the fork in his hand, resolved to wait for the dance to end so that he could enjoy his meal without the show.

Belly dancing, as well as flamenco dancing, was an art in Cordoba. With the island nation's proximity to both Spain and Egypt, many people studied the art forms. After centuries of effort, modern Cordovians had perfected and fused the styles together into something that was unique to their people. It was a style Alex enjoyed. But not at the moment.

The dancer wiggled her hips and belly in beat to the percussion. The woman was talented. Alex would give her that. He just was less interested in her show and more interested in the cooling dish that awaited his first bite.

In the meantime, Alex hovered over his food like a caveman unwilling to share his bounty. In truth, he simply didn't want hip sweat to land on his plate as an unwanted additive.

"Your hips don't lie, dear girl," said Zhi.

There were two dancers on his side of the table. The young duke held his hands up and swayed in his seat to the beat of the dancers' moves. As the dancers wiggled faster and faster, Zhi reached over to tuck a few bills in the dancer's coin-lined sarong. He stuffed a fistful of bills down the other two girls' costumes. Unfortunately, his arms didn't quite reach the dancer on Alex's side.

"Alex, be a prince and show the girl our appreciation."

Alex rolled his eyes at his oldest friend as he stuffed the bills in his utensil-less hand. When Alex had suggested the place, it was for the food. The only reason Zhi came was for the entertainment.

It had been a compromise of sorts. The two friends had hardly had any chance to catch up with Zhi taking over his ancestral estate now that his father was ill. This night for him was about letting his hair down from all of his newfound responsibilities.

Alex had not been there for his friend in the last few weeks. He'd been off traveling, and now he was about to start his own business. And he was engaged.

He'd almost asked Jan if she'd wanted to come along to this guys' night. Just to try the dish. In the end, he decided it was best not to bring his fiancée to a gentleman's club, even if it was on the posh side of town.

Alex doubted the pie maker would enjoy the atmosphere, but he was certain she'd enjoy the dish. He was certain he would enjoy the dish once he actually got a taste of it. To do that, he'd need to get rid of the dancer.

He took the money Zhi gave him. But instead of stuffing the money in the girl's clothing, Alex placed it in her hand. With that done, Alex turned to the fork in his hand and the bite that was still on its tines. But there was something tugging at his other hand.

He looked up to see the dancer's face close to his. She

leaned in and kissed his cheek before taking the cash. On cue, a camera flashed.

A few days ago, Alex wouldn't have cared. He knew the press' narrative about him. He knew they didn't care to change it. But after Jan had come to his defense the other day, Alex wanted to play a new role.

The woman bent her body down as though to sit in Alex's lap. Alex shifted, still not dropping the morsel of food on his fork. He brought her down next to him in an empty seat. Then he plopped the food into his mouth.

Pulling the tines slowly from his mouth, he groaned in delight. He held up the index finger of his free hand to the girl while he took a moment to enjoy the complex flavors. The garlic and cilantro hit him first. Just beneath the sweet oniony flavor was a layer of pepper and lemon. And was that the subtle hint of ginger? Truly a work of art. He was definitely going back to speak to the chef. Perhaps he might even steal the man away to come and work for him and Jan.

As he used his knife and fork to craft another perfect bite, he addressed the woman waiting beside him. "How much are they paying you for the picture?"

The dancer hesitated. Her gaze flickered across the way. It was the same direction that the flash had originated.

"Tell me the number," said Alex. "I'll double it. If you'll go away."

Her gaze went wide with greed. She told him a number Alex knew was a markup on the market price for a scandalous photo of him. He didn't care. He opened his wallet and peeled off a few bills. He gave them to the girl with a hand shake, and she was off.

"What's gotten into you?" Zhi asked.

"I'm engaged." Alex lifted his fork and devoured the bite.

"Does that mean you can't have a little fun?" asked Zhi. "Don't get me wrong, I like Jan. She's far too good for you."

Alex ignored his friend, especially since he was right. Jan was too good for him. But he found himself wanting to be a better man, a man who deserved her. He decided that instead of arguing, he'd turn the tables.

"What's gotten into *you*?" Alex shot back. "I was speaking with Carlisle the other day."

The soon to be Baron of Balansya rounded out their threesome. The three men had grown up together, gone to the same schools, and eschewed the same responsibilities together. Though Carlisle had always been the one behind his family's business success as early as his teen years.

"He told me he was worried about you," Alex continued. "Said you haven't been yourself. Is it your father? Is it worse than we believed?"

"The man's old. His title and his power can't stop the inevitable."

Zhi wouldn't meet Alex's gaze. That's how Alex knew something else was wrong. But he and Zhi had never been the type of men to cry on each other's shoulders.

No, they saved that for when they got drunk. Then they'd blubber on, confident that the other would forget the next morning. They never forgot. But they also never spoke of it.

"You always said you'd never marry," said Zhi. "And now you're engaged to a pie maker? I repeat; what's gotten into you?"

Alex opened his mouth, but his tongue was tied. Just as he couldn't lie to his blood brother, he couldn't seem to lie to his chosen brother. The problem was Alex wasn't sure what the lie was any longer. Was the lie that he was engaged to Jan? Or was the lie that he no longer wanted to get married?

"You really like this girl?" said Zhi.

"Yeah." Alex could admit to that truth. "I do."

He looked down at the dish. It made him think of Jan; how well the sweet and the spice of the two of them paired together. Two pairings that didn't appear to fit together, but once paired, they made perfect, palatable sense.

"We're good together," Alex said. "She believes in me."

"I believe she will be good for you," said Zhi. "You know, for a while there, I thought it was a ploy to get your inheritance."

Instead of looking up at his friend, Alex shoveled the last bite of the dish into his mouth. The last bite was even better than the first.

"But it's not. You're really going to do this? You're going to get married?"

Once upon a time, that very thought would break Alex out into hives. He had never wanted to marry. He'd always wanted to make his own way in the world. The thought settled over him now like a warm cup of tea. The thought of spending the rest of his life with Jan felt … right.

"You'll pick me as your best man," said Zhi. "Your brother will have your stag party at the opera."

Alex laughed, knowing that his best friend was probably right about Leo's party planning. But picking a best man was the least of his concerns. He had to figure out how he would convince his fake fiancée to consider giving their pretend relationship a real shot.

CHAPTER TWENTY

"He wants to take you on a romantic getaway!" Esme's high-pitched squeal sent a vibration through Jan's wineglass.

"It's not romantic." Jan pinched the bridge between her nose to regain her sense of equilibrium. "It's work."

"A prince wants to whisk you away for the weekend on his private yacht to a small town in Spain for work." Esme used air quotes. Her dark eyes sparkled with light as she stared down her best friend.

"He doesn't need an excuse to take me anywhere. He is my fake fiancé."

"Is that what he said?"

Jan paused in taking a sip of her wine. Alex hadn't used the word fake in a while. He hadn't even used the word work the other day. "He said that I was his fiancée, and he didn't need a reason to wine and dine me."

Esme pressed her lips together and tapped her feet to the beat of Jan's racing heart. Her friend looked as though she were about to burst into a red heart-shaped balloon and float away.

Jan sat her wineglass down, uncertain she could manage its weight any longer. She got up and began pacing the room. They were in Esme's waiting room. She was supposed to be interviewing more ladies-in-waiting, but she'd had them wait while she took an audience with Jan.

"It's not like that, Essie ... not really."

Jan thought back to the other day when he'd kissed her when they were at the restaurant under fire from a photographer's camera. She'd lied and told him the coast wasn't clear so that she could have another taste of him. Alex hadn't had his back to the window. They'd both been standing perpendicular to it.

But he'd asked her to look. Meanwhile, he'd only had eyes for her. He hadn't confirmed what she'd told him. It had been as if he'd wanted a reason to keep going as much as she had.

And, oh boy, did Jan want to keep going. She'd never been kissed like that. Like she was a tasting dish, not just an amuse-bouche. She'd felt like she was the main course and dessert rolled into one. She was sure Alex kissed like that on the regular. A man didn't get that good without practice and a lot of it.

"I don't think it's like that for him, Jan."

Jan sat down and reached for her wineglass. She tipped the glass and threw it all down her throat. The burn was just what she needed. She could not fall for this man. It would be such a cliché rolled into a disaster.

A fake relationship where, over the course of events, one party falls for the other. Alex hadn't fallen for her. She was sure of it.

Pretty sure.

Somewhat certain.

She glanced at the morning paper, and there was her proof. He'd gone out last night, and his exploits were splashed on the front page. There he was at a gentleman's club getting a kiss on the cheek from a scantily clad dancer.

Jan's eyes traveled down the picture. In Alex's other hand, he held a fork. Her gaze traveled to the dish on the table before him. The picture was in color, and the plate of food looked delicious even in print. She wondered what it was? What it tasted like?

"That doesn't mean anything," Esme said, yanking the paper from the table and tossing it into a bin.

Jan could beg to differ. She had no claim on Alex outside of their business arrangement. She supposed she should tell him to keep a low profile in his exploits so that she didn't get embarrassed.

But at some point in this venture, she would be the one to get embarrassed. They were going to call it off. It didn't matter who did the calling off. She'd be alone afterward, and Alex would be gallivanting around with women like always. Just like it had been with Chris.

How had she gotten herself into the same situation? For the rest of her life, she'd have to watch the man she had feelings for go off with other women. And none of them would be her.

She dropped her face into her hands.

"Jan? Honey, what is it?"

"It's a disaster. I can't believe I made the same mistake."

"What mistake?" Esme tugged at her wrists.

Jan refused to let the tears fall. She'd made a business decision. She knew how this was supposed to end. It was just that she never thought she'd feel more than wariness for Alex.

But then there had been those kisses. There was the way he'd held her. The way they cooked together and mixed spices. She'd never had that with anyone. For a cook, that was the height of intimacy.

"You have feelings for him?" said Esme. "Don't you?"

Jan nodded her head, still hiding her face.

"Sweetie, I think he has feelings for you too."

Jan dropped her hands then. She huffed in exasperation at Esme. The woman had always excelled in seeing things that weren't there. One day, Esme's imagination would get her in trouble. But seeing as the woman had a king and a castle, it didn't look like that day was coming any time soon.

"I was talking to Leo," she went on, "and he said he'd

never seen Alex look at a woman the way he looked at you when you came to his defense the other day."

Jan shook her head. She would not be pulled into one of Esme's fairy tales. They may have worked the one time for Esme. They would never work for plain girls like Jan.

"Really, Jan, think about it. He chose you to cook with him. He chose you to partner with him. He chose you for this fake engagement ploy. Leo would give him the money. Heck, I would give you two the money. Did you know that being a queen is an actual job with an annual salary? My point is that nothing of those options, which he knew were open to him, would tie you to him. I think subconsciously, he wants you."

Could Esme be right? Jan didn't know what to think? She wasn't even sure what she wanted?

Did she want Alex to be falling for her? She had sworn she'd never get married. That she'd never tie her life to anyone else. But she'd signed on the line to be partners with Alex, a business partnership that she hoped would last a lifetime. Did she want that partnership to extend outside of the kitchen?

Jan thought back to that kiss the other day, and her lips tingled. Her heart fluttered. There was her answer.

"But what about the paper?" Jan inclined her head to the paper in the trash.

Esme sighed and retrieve the crumbled paper. "I want you to look at something. Look in his eyes." Esme pointed to the creased and crinkled Alex on paper. "He looks annoyed, not amused. In fact, look at his hand. He has a fork. He was eating, and she interrupted his dinner."

Jan had seen the food, but not the annoyance in his gaze. Even now, she focused more on the dish than on Alex. There was a bit of jealousy that rose. But she realized the envy wasn't over the girl.

It was over the dish. Jan was jealous that he was eating someone else's food. And without her.

"I think you should talk to him," said Esme. "Tell him how you feel."

The mere thought of the possibility of rejection made Jan's spine ache. The idea of making herself that vulnerable to another person scared her. Could she trust Alex with her heart?

She'd trusted him with her livelihood, her future security, and her career. Those had long since mattered more than her heart.

"Jan, whether you want to believe it or not, there's a thing between you two. I saw it with my own eyes back during the pie competition."

He'd kissed her then too. It was just casual that time. It had been nothing like the way he'd kissed her the other day.

The kiss after the pie making competition had been a firm press to the lips; a congratulations. The kiss the other day had been one where he'd savored her like she was the last bite of a brownie. Alex did love chocolate.

"I'll talk to him," she agreed.

Esme squealed and danced in her seat. "We're going to be real sisters. Royal sisters."

Jan sighed. Esme might be ready for her friend to walk down the aisle, but Jan wasn't in a hurry. She would talk to Alex about the thin line between fiction and reality in their relationship. But she didn't have to talk to him right now. She had time.

lex spread the plans for the restaurant over a worktable in the kitchen. Already, contractors were measuring floors and ordering supplies. Interior designers were assembling color swatches and had furniture catalogues opened in the other room. The three backers had already wired the first installment of investments. As Alex updated them on the progress, they were set to send the full balance of what they'd promised.

It was all coming together. He was going to have everything he had never dared to dream of, including a few things he'd never thought he'd wish for.

Like Jan.

The fake engagement was turning into something very real. Something he'd never thought he'd wanted. But he never thought he'd wanted fried grasshoppers until he'd tried the chapulines in Mexico.

Now that he'd had a taste of Jan, he wanted another

bite, another nibble, another sip of her every day. Possibly, even, for the rest of his life.

No. Definitely for the rest of his life. He didn't like the thought of a day without Jan. A day without her smile. An afternoon without a hard-won grin from her lips. A night without cooking next to her and then dining beside her.

But Alex wasn't prepared to tell her any of that today. He was still getting used to the new feelings himself. He knew Jan had a hang up when it came to marriage. He'd never abandon her, not at the altar, not in life. He'd take these few months of their fake engagement to show her that. He'd wine and dine and romance her until she knew there was nowhere else she wanted to be but inside his arms.

With that thought, Alex felt giddy. He felt as though he were at a candy store that served all his favorite treats. The best part was that he and Jan could make all of those treats in real life.

Before he could have any of his just desserts, he had to focus on the business at hand. They would be serving a preview meal for some of Cordoba's most popular food critics. For the first time in his life, Alex cared about getting a good report in the newspapers. What the critics said the night of the dinner could make or break their future.

But he wasn't worried. Not in the slightest. He believed that much in his little pie maker and her abilities. He didn't hear her enter the room, but he turned and there she was.

Jan was dressed in simple jeans and a T-shirt. She looked breathtaking. Literally. Alex forgot how to breathe for a moment as she walked toward him.

But as she got closer, he noticed that her face looked different. Gone was the no nonsense certainty. She was looking down at the floor, not up at him. She twisted and chewed at her bottom lip. Her hands rubbed against the sides of her jeans. She shoved them into her pockets. Then took them out and crossed her arms.

She was fidgeting.

"Hey," he said.

"Hey," she parroted. She took a deep breath, as though to steady herself, and looked up at him. Her gaze even seemed cloudy with indecision.

"How are you this morning?"

"Good. Good," she said. "How was your night?"

Before he could answer, she cringed. She brought the heel of her palm to her forehead and cursed under her breath.

"I'm sorry," she groaned. "I didn't mean that. I meant, how did you sleep?" She groaned again, turning away from him and pinching the bridge of her nose. "Not that I'm accusing you of sleeping with anyone."

"Jan? What are you talking about?"

"I saw the papers."

"The papers?"

"It's none of my business. We're just business partners."

Oh, those papers. They must have printed the photos with Alex at the club the other night with the dancer. He made his way over to Jan on quick feet. He didn't care what anyone else might think of those photos, but he had to clear that up with her.

Jan held out her hands before he could get to her. "I just have to ask one thing of you."

"Anything."

"Can you be more discreet with other women? I am your fake fiancée and—"

"Nothing happened."

"You don't have to explain." She shut her eyes as though shutting out his voice, and the reality he was trying to detail for her.

"Actually, I do."

Her arms were down at her sides, and he was able to sweep her into his embrace. She gasped when his arms came around her. Her eyes opened wide with surprise. Her lips parted, and he breathed in her sweet breath. He nearly forgot what he was trying to say as he fought not to take her lips.

"I was with Zhi, remember him?"

Jan nodded. A few of the clouds scattered from her gaze.

"He wanted to put money in the dancer's skirt. I was closest to her."

Alex's right hand came to rest on Jan's hip. Unlike the

dancer last night, Jan was fully clothed. Not an inch of her midriff was showing. She was the most desirable woman Alex had ever encountered.

"I saw the flash go off," he continued. "It was a set up. The dancer was in on it. More fodder for their headlines of the playboy prince. I was only there for the food."

"I did see your hand on the fork. What was it?"

"What was what?" Alex's mind was on Jan's hands which were resting on his chest. He wondered if she could feel how his heart raced at her touch.

"What was the dish? It looked amazing."

"It was delicious. It was Marrakchia, a Moroccan dish. I had it when I traveled there a couple of years ago. The chef did a good job, but having it on the streets of Marrakesh is the only way to go. We'll travel there soon."

"After our trips to France and Spain?" She grinned.

"Anywhere you want to go."

Jan's gaze went to the floor again, and she tugged at her lip. But this time, there were no clouds of doubt in her gaze. There was no worrying of her lips.

"So, you believe me then?"

Jan's lips tugged into a sheepish grin. "I was honestly more jealous that you were eating without me than I was that you were entertaining another woman."

Alex threw back his head and laughed, but he didn't loosen his hold on Jan. He gazed down at her, completely transfixed by the woman with a delectable palate that he wanted to taste again and again.

"I wasn't with another woman," he said. "I wouldn't

do that to you. Your reputation means a lot to me. I'm going to protect it as best I can. But they'll try more things. Photoshop is my biggest enemy."

"I'm sorry you have to put up with this. That people don't see you the way I do."

They were standing so close together. They were breathing the same air. Their chests rose and fell in unison.

"How do you see me?" he asked.

She looked down at the floor again as though unwilling to show him the depths of her emotions. "I love how passionate you are about food. How excited you get to try something new. How you'll pick a dish apart and then want to put it back together but make it better."

"You make me sound like you." He reached up and brushed a stray hair behind her ear. He promised his lips that they'd make the same trek soon. "We are pretty much alike, aren't we?"

She'd lifted her gaze finally. There was admiration in her eyes. It was a far cry from adoration. There were facts in the flecks of her eyes, not conjecture. Jan knew him. He knew her.

He knew she'd had strawberries for breakfast. He could smell them on her breath. He'd had a couple too. What he didn't know is how they'd tasted on her tongue.

"Jan?"

"Hmmm?"

"I was thinking—"

"That's where we always run into trouble." She grinned.

"We should probably go on a few actual dates since we are engaged." Alex traced another path from her temple to her ear though there were no strands of hair out of place.

"You mean for the press?" Her head tilted ever so slightly until her cheek was resting in his palm.

"I don't care about the press."

"You don't?"

He shook his head. But she didn't see. Her eyes had fluttered closed as her head rested in his hand. He was so close that his nose stole an Eskimo kiss. "I like eating with you. I like sharing new experiences with you. I like being with you."

"Me too."

"You busy tonight?"

Her eyes opened and her gaze fixed on him. She looked as hungry as he felt.

"Yes," she sighed. "I am."

He frowned.

"So are you. We have to prepare for the critic's dinner. That's why we're here right now."

"Right. I forgot."

She smiled, and it lit up her whole face. Had he ever seen her smile like that? He wanted to taste it. His eyes dipped to her lips.

Jan wet her lower lip. Alex could read the signs. That

motion was a clear sign meaning she knew he wanted to kiss her.

When she held her place, he knew she wouldn't pull away, she was going to let him kiss her. He wasn't going to have to wait as long as he'd planned to win her over. He might decide the battle at that moment. A loud crash sounded from the other room, tearing them apart.

Alex groaned. "Hopefully, the contractors won't ruin the place before we get a chance to open it. I'll go see what they're up to."

"I'm gonna head down the street to the market to find some fresh ingredients."

"I'll come find you when I'm done with them, okay?"

She nodded, her cheeks pinking, but she held his gaze as she went out the back door of the kitchens. Alex rushed to the other room to get the contractors in order. The sooner he did, the sooner he could get back to Jan.

CHAPTER TWENTY-TWO

*J*an kept pressing her fingers to her lips. She'd been doing that for the past few days every day since her first kiss with Alex. If she were honest with herself, she'd admit she'd been doing it for a month since the very first time he'd pressed his lips to hers.

With each subsequent kiss, he'd fed a fire in her. Now she was burning up inside. The only time she felt relief was when she was in his arms.

Oh, boy, did she have it bad.

She was happy to know that she wasn't alone. Alex hadn't professed his undying love for her back in the kitchen, but he'd made it clear that he was feeling something too. Alex, the uncatchable catch was somehow, miraculously, unexplainably hooked on her.

On her; Jan. The plain pie maker. Jan the jilted. Jan had a suspicion she wouldn't be jilted this time.

No, he hadn't promised her forever. Not a love kind of forever. But he'd promised her a business kind of forever. The romance, or whatever it was blossoming between them, might last a few weeks, a few months. They might even have a few years.

Jan knew it was more than Alex had ever planned to give anyone. It was more than she'd ever thought she'd wanted for herself.

And she did want it.

With him.

Standing at the farmer's table, Jan squeezed the tomato in her hand. It gave. Much like her resolve to give up on love.

"Excuse me, miss," said a fellow shopper to her left. "Can you help me choose? I'm a terrible cook."

Jan turned to face the woman. Helping the culinary-challenged was a favorite hobby of hers. But the moment she looked into the woman's shrewd gaze, Jan reared back.

"I have nothing to say to you." Jan put the ripe tomato in her basket and gave the reporter, Lila Drake, her back.

Lila raced in her heels to keep up with Jan. The pavement was cobblestones. Jan hoped the woman's spike heel got caught in a crack and broke her back.

"Did you see this morning's papers?"

Jan remained mute as she marched on to the next crate. She gave her full concentration to the long, orange carrots neatly placed in rows.

"I just need a quote from the would-be bride."

"Would be?"

"Oh, come on, honey. You don't really expect Prince Alex, the playboy prince, to actually get to the aisle? From what I hear, you have some experience with that."

Jan bit the inside of her cheek. She knew what the reporter was doing. Trying to get a rise out of her so that she could get a scoop.

Jan gave her a sweet smile. "Guess you'll just have to wait and see, won't you. And if it happens, I'll be sure and contact your competition to give them all the details."

Lila snorted. "Right, because a handsome prince is going to marry a jilted, plain-looking, pie maker from New Jersey. That's how the storybooks go."

Jan felt the sting. She wanted to say it wasn't true. She wanted to say that there was a thing between her and Alex. But she wouldn't believe it.

"He's never getting married," said Lila. "He's just going to live off the people's tax money until he dies. This is clearly a stunt to detract from that. But everyone loves an underdog story; the dog being you. I can easily make you into a sympathetic character if you play ball."

Jan squeezed the carrot in her hand. Unlike the tomato, the vegetable didn't give. It snapped.

She had had enough. She was used to people talking and believing poorly of her. But Alex was a good person inside and out. He hid behind a facade so that he could go around the world making people's lives better. And people like Lila Drake did nothing but spew negativity and lies.

"You were there in Nairobi weren't you?" said Jan. "You know he didn't hook up with that actress or model or whatever."

"Oh, honey, he hooked up with a model, believe you me."

Jan grit her teeth. "You saw what he did in the village."

'With the green house thing? So what?"

"Why not report on that?"

"Because no one wants to read about a do-good prince," Lila said as though Jan were the most naïve schoolgirl in the world. "Women don't dream about a charitable prince. Notice how little press King Leo gets. Every girl wants the bad boy."

"The people should know the truth of their prince. That he doesn't spend extravagantly. When he goes off on these trips, he's always helping the less fortunate. That he barely spends a dime. Others just gift him services because they want to use his name. Everyone just wants to use him."

"But not you?" said Lila.

"Of course not."

"So you're not after his inheritance? I'd bet you could open many restaurants with that money."

It was a little too on the nose, and Jan had to settle her face before she spoke. Unfortunately, Lila caught the subtle shift.

"Wait a minute, this is about his inheritance isn't it?"

"Wrong again," said Jan. "It's actually not. Alex isn't using his own money. We have investors."

Lila shook her head. "Something doesn't add up."

"Yeah, your investigative skills. There's no story here."

Lila ignored Jan and began counting the facts on her fingers. "A prince who said he'd never marry suddenly shows up with a fiancée who's a virtual nobody."

"Hey!"

"The two of you are opening a restaurant, but you're using other people's money to do it, even though the prince could have his own funds if only he married. Wait. That's it. You're scamming the investors."

"We are not." How could she add up all those facts and get the wrong sum? "Alex would never do such a thing."

"True or not, it's the angle that's going to get printed." Lila whipped out a cell phone and began texting.

Jan stood rooted in her spot. There was nothing she could do to stop the salacious reporter. It was just like Alex had said. Once they got their narrative, that's what they'd run with. They'd ignore anything to the contrary. All Jan could do was warn Alex.

CHAPTER TWENTY-THREE

lex shook hands with the last contractor as the man walked out the front door. He just needed to wash his hands, grab his jacket, and then head out to find Jan. But heading back into the kitchen to retrieve his coat, he turned and stared.

The dining area was essentially a blank slate. But Alex saw it clearly. He saw the guests lining up out the door. He saw tourists gaping at the finery as they took a seat. He saw locals toasting at the bar after a long day's work. He would be at the front of the house, commandeering it all.

Jan would be at the back in the kitchen of her dreams. Every spice from around the world would be within reach of her fingertips.

He'd taste every dish before it went out. Not to check up on her, but because he wanted to taste whatever came from her imagination. But that would be right after he tasted her lips. In fact, he doubted he'd ever use a dining utensil again. From now on, he'd only eat food straight from her fingertips.

Pride swelled in his chest as he headed for the door. He wondered if he could push the open date up sooner. This was an accomplishment he did want to shout about. He wanted the whole world to know about what he and Jan could do together.

Before he could pull the door open to find the woman he wanted to share the spotlight with, she raced up the steps and flung herself into his arms. She was shaking, trembling. Alex held her tightly and brought her inside the safety of the nest they were building together.

"Jan? What is it? What's wrong?"

She sobbed into his chest, not showing him her face. Alex's heart cracked, threatening to splinter in two at the sounds. Whatever happened, whoever did this, he'd open up the dungeons to them.

"I've screwed it all up," Jan hiccoughed.

"What, my darling? Please, tell me what's happened, and I promise I'll fix it."

He brought her tighter into his arms, tucking her head beneath his chin. He rubbed his hands at her back, trying to sooth the cries out of her spine. It took long moments, but soon her cries died down, and her breathing steadied.

When Jan looked up at him, anger sparkled in her blue eyes. "That reporter, Lila Drake, cornered me while I was out shopping."

Cold dread washed through Alex's entire body. It was a lucky thing that he held Jan in his arms. Otherwise, he'd race out of there to find the tabloid tattler and give her a piece of his mind. He no longer cared what they said about him, but Jan was off limits.

"I was trying to defend you," Jan said. "But I slipped up. She figured it out. The inheritance and the investors. She knows. Pretty soon, everyone will know that the engagement is fake."

Alex closed his eyes and breathed a sigh. This was his worst nightmare. So, why was he so calm?

He brushed the tears away from Jan's eyes until he saw her clearly. There was nothing fake about their engagement. Unless they counted their own denials of how they felt for each other.

"Alex, I'm so sorry."

"Don't be."

"I should've kept my mouth shut. I tried, but then she went on and on about how you were just a playboy living off the citizen's dime, and it wasn't true."

He leaned down and pressed his forehead to hers. "I don't care what they say about me. I only care what you think about me."

"I don't believe any of it. I mean, I did. But that was before I got to know you, the real you."

She sighed and the morning strawberry sweetness still lingered on her breath. Alex realized he had never gotten his taste test.

"But now I've ruined everything," she said, bitterness

lacing her tongue. "When Lila Drake prints that story, the investors will find out. They'll think we scammed them. They'll pull out."

That caught Alex's attention. He hadn't considered that bit of fall out.

"I think I should just leave," she said.

Jan gave a tug, but Alex wouldn't relinquish his hold on her.

"I think it's for the best," she continued. "The press will forget about me. You can still open the restaurant. Alex and Esme will invest if you don't want to use the inheritance. You can hire another chef and—"

"No." His voice was firm. "I won't hear of it. This place is nothing without you. I am nothing without you."

"But I've crushed your dream."

She hadn't. Not even slightly. He would run a food cart so long as she was beside him. For now, he laced their fingers together, down to the webbing until it felt like they were one.

"I've dreamed of opening a place like this all my life," he said. "But I never thought I could do it until I met you. We do this together or not at all."

"You want me to stay?" she asked. "As your business partner?"

"I want you ..." He swallowed a huge lump in his throat.

The rest of the words were right on the tip of his lips, but they wouldn't come out. She'd been so ready to walk away from him. Could she feel the same way about him as he did about her if she were so ready to give him up?

"I want you," he tried again, "however I can keep you."

Jan gasped at his words. Ever the opportunist, Alex took advantage. He pulled her to him. His lips brushed lightly over hers before he broke away and led them out the front door.

The light kiss wasn't enough, but it would do. They had work to do. There still was a chance they could save the restaurant and their dream. But they'd have to move fast.

CHAPTER TWENTY-FOUR

The King of Cordoba slammed the morning paper down on his desk. The edges of the thin parchment trembled under his fingers. Though the paper was lightweight, its words fired heavy artillery.

Jan flinched at the sound of Leo's palm on the wood, and at the angry, belligerent picture they'd captured of her.

Her lips were pulled from her teeth in a snarl as she faced off against that awful reporter. One hand was raised, a finger raised in the woman's face as though she were telling her off. Well, that part at least, they'd gotten right.

Jan had told Lila Drake off. She'd tried to make the woman see reason, see the truth. But like every other story the scandal pusher published, this story twisted and contorted the facts until it wasn't even reality.

"This is an unmitigated disaster," said Leo. "It's the worst jam you've gotten yourself into."

Those comments were directed at Alex. Just as Jan wouldn't stand by and let the reporter paint Alex in a negative light, she wouldn't allow his brother to do it either.

"Alex didn't do this," said Jan. "It was that horrible reporter. I told her the truth about him. She knew the truth and still all she wanted to do was print lies."

"But this isn't a lie." Leo held up the paper.

The headline read *Flambé Fiancée*. The story went on to detail how Jan was the mastermind behind a plan to swindle Alex out of his inheritance. Lila was cruel characterizing Jan as a brain with no beauty. The words had hurt, not because they were true, but because they would be so easy for others to believe.

Jan had never been some great beauty. It made sense that the only reason Alex had agreed to marry her was out of trickery. She supposed she should be pleased that she was portrayed as smart enough to pull it off.

"Not a word of that about Jan is true." Alex's voice was a low growl. He stood behind her chair. His hand, which had been resting at the top of the chair close to the nape of her neck without touching it, tensed.

Esme sat beside Jan, holding her hand in a tight, supportive grip. Outside, at the palace gates, the press had gathered. Out Leo's office window, Jan could see their flashing lights in the distance. They were quite literally storming the castle.

"I'm referring to the part where the two of you have no plans to get married," said Leo.

Jan felt Alex stiffen beside her. She might have changed her stance on marriage, but she hadn't thought he had. She knew he never wanted to walk down the aisle.

But now it was all ruined. If they continued the engagement, everyone would speculate that they were only in it for the money. If they broke it off, it would confirm it as well. What were they going to do?

"We can salvage this," Alex said quietly.

Jan looked over her shoulder so that she could see his face. Gone was the mischievous glint to his dark eyes. He looked tired, resolute.

"I made you a promise," he said, "and I intend to keep it."

"What are you talking about?" asked Leo.

"She gave up everything to try to make this work. She left her home, her family, her business," shouted Alex, prowling over to Leo's desk. The two brothers stood toe to toe. "We were never going to need the inheritance. This is a good, sound investment. We are a good, sound investment."

The two brothers glared at each other. Jan's insides twisted. Everything was ruined; the business, the relationship that was just getting started with Alex, and the relationship he had with his brother.

Instead of things coming to blows, Leo reached out to his brother and brought Alex into his arms.

"You should've come to me," Leo growled. "Don't you know you can always come to me?"

"I didn't think you'd believe ..." Alex let the words trail off.

"You didn't think I believed in you." Leo broke the hug and held his brother at arm's length so he could look directly into his eyes. "I'm ashamed to say there's a possibility you may have been right."

Alex looked down at the ground and sighed. When he raised his head, there wasn't defeat in his gaze. "That's fair."

"I would've believed in Jan."

Alex gave his brother a punch in the shoulder. But, despite the levity of the moment, they were still in a world of trouble. All eyes rested on the opened paper still on Leo's desk.

"We can still make this work," said Alex.

"How?" said Esme, speaking for the first time since seeing the paper.

"I just need to step out of the limelight for a while," said Alex.

"You're leaving me?" Jan rose, letting go of her best friend's hand. Without Esme, she realized there was nothing tethering her, and her knees nearly buckled.

"No." Alex came to her, wrapping her up in his arms. "Yes but no."

Jan searched his gaze. There was remorse in his dark eyes. But there was more, something deeper. It was the same look he'd given her the other day when he asked her out to dinner. The same look he'd had when he'd leaned in to kiss her when they were alone without any cameras.

Jan wasn't an expert in reality. She'd seen enough romantic comedies to think she knew what she was looking at. It looked like real, live desire. It looked the way the hero looked at the heroine in the last few moments of the movie before declaring his undying love. Was Alex about to declare his undying love for her? Jan desperately wanted to turn to Esme to get her bestie to give her assessment of the potentially declarative look of love in Alex's eyes.

"I think we should break up," he said.

It was déjà vu. She'd been here before. It was different words but the same feeling.

Her heart was in her feet. Her head was light. Her legs unsteady.

She'd had to take a seat after Chris had told her he was leaving her. She'd been standing at the back of the church in her wedding gown, ready to walk down the aisle toward him. He'd been holding another woman's hand as he spoke to her. Jan had had only the wall to hold her up.

She was in the center of Leo's office. The wall was more than a yard away. So how was she still upright?

Alex's arms were still around her. In fact, he was holding her even tighter. As though he never wanted to let her go. But hadn't he just broken up with her?

"I'll march out there right now and tell them all that

the plan was my idea," he was saying. "Because it was my idea. We'll cast you as the sympathetic girl done wrong."

"No," she said. But her voice was barely above a whisper. It didn't matter. Alex went on as though he didn't hear her.

"Leo will cast me out for such a dastardly deed."

"I'll do no such thing," Leo said, but Alex ignored him as well.

"I'll step out of the limelight for awhile," Alex continued. "Not that it'll keep the wolves at bay. If I run, they'll follow me. But that means they'll forget Jan. Your reputation will be saved. That's what's important here."

"No," Jan said again, her voice stronger this time. "You didn't do anything wrong. You shouldn't have to run."

Alex cupped her cheek, rubbing his thumb over her lower lip. "I only care that you see me for who I am."

"I do."

"No." He tilted her head back so that he could peer directly down into her eyes. "I don't think you do. This is an entirely new me. I feel like a new man with you."

Jan's heart was overflowing like a pie with too much yeast. Emotion spilled out of her eyes and landed on her heated cheeks. "I don't want you to leave me."

"I'm not leaving you." He wiped her tears away with his thumb as he held her firmly to him. "Well, I mean I am. But I'm not."

"You're giving a lot of mixed messages here, Alex."

"Let me be clear. I'm going to go on one of my trips. Maybe to a desert or to the Arctic. Wherever I can that will make any press which follows me miserable. You'll stay here and open the restaurant as planned. We'll talk every day. You'll be sick of me by the time I drag myself back here with my tail between my legs to beg your forgiveness in a huge spectacle and plead with you to take me back. Deal?"

Jan didn't want to make a new deal. She didn't want to be left alone in any capacity. The only pact she wanted was one where she and Alex stayed side by side. And kisses. She wanted a deal with lots of kisses.

"This is touching and all, but you're missing the obvious answer," said Leo. "Just get married. You'll have the money. The press will be proven wrong. Everyone gets what they want."

Jan changed her mind. That was the deal she wanted. Exactly as Leo had laid it out.

Alex sighed, dropping his chin to his chest, and Jan's heart sank. Everyone wouldn't get what they wanted. Alex didn't want to get married.

He may have wanted to date her. Maybe even for a long time. But forever as a couple wasn't in the cards. Which meant there was no reason for Alex to take the fall.

Alex planted a kiss on her forehead. Then he turned to face his brother. As Alex and Leo continued to argue over the details, with Esme playing referee, Jan slipped out of the office.

She headed down the hall and out the front door. Taking the long walk down the drive to the gate, she saw the press. They were all lined up, talking to each other.

Her sensible shoes crunched over the gravel. She was sure they couldn't hear her through their own chatting and laughter. But yards away, like predators sensing prey, they heard her.

In unison, their heads turned. Their eyes widened in surprise. Then they wet their lips, held up their cameras and microphones, and the frenzy began.

Jan was still yards away. She had a distance yet to march down the aisle toward the gathered crowd. Instantly, she was transported back to her wedding day, standing at the end of the aisle.

Jan knew where Alex was. She knew why he wasn't by her side. She knew that everything he was doing was to protect her from this very scenario. And yet, here she was throwing herself into the lion's den to protect him.

If that wasn't love, she didn't know what was.

She couldn't freeze now. She had to face this and tell them all the truth. Jan turned to face the beasts who were all hungry for a scoop. She put one foot in front of the other and then another.

It was slow progress, but finally, she was standing before them. Now she just had to force the words from her mouth.

A hush swept over the crowd as they awaited her first words. She waited with breathless anticipation as well. She only hoped the words would come out soon.

CHAPTER TWENTY-FIVE

"I'm sorry, but marriage is the only way," said Leo.

Alex hadn't argued. Not because he thought that what his brother was saying was a fallacy. He knew that if he simply went out there and reconfirmed his engagement to Jan, the press would leave them alone. For a while. But then something else would come up. It always did.

The reason Alex didn't argue with his brother was that he agreed with Leo's statement. Marriage was the only way forward that he wanted to move with Jan.

Alex wanted more than a business arrangement with the pie maker. He wanted more than just her partnership in the kitchen. He wanted to be with her in each and every room of their very own house after they closed the restaurant each day. He wanted to make her breakfast every morning. He wanted to take her with him on his culinary adventures.

"A real engagement that leads to a legal marriage is the only way I can see to save your reputation," said Leo.

"There's no need for investors," Esme said, standing beside her husband. "We'll invest."

Alex opened his mouth to turn the offer down.

"Alex," Esme sighed. "That's what families do. We support each other, especially when it's our dreams."

Alex looked to his brother.

Leo put his arm around his wife and nodded. "I believe in you. I want to see you work at your passion, and you're clearly passionate about this."

"I am," said Alex.

"You never wanted any part of the family business. But you are my business. You are my family. I want in on this. If nothing more than to show you that I believe in you."

Alex took in a deep breath, but his heart was too filled with emotion. He had to blow the air back out. It was an offer he'd never considered. Now that it was on the table, he couldn't refuse.

He lifted his head and stretched out his hand to his brother. Leo took Alex's hand and pulled him in for a hug. It had been a long time since Alex had been held by a member of his family. His father was always too distant and aloof. Leo had tried to walk in his father's footsteps early, but Alex had gotten a few hugs back when he was small. He was now coming to realize Leo's rare embraces had meant the world to him.

The embrace ended all too quickly. Both brothers fidgeted, not quite meeting the others' gaze now that there was air between them. Esme rolled her eyes, but she grinned, clearly pleased with the outcome.

"I know you never wanted anything arranged," Leo said, "but the two of you get on. You have similar interests. And frankly, I don't think you could do better."

Leo looked pointedly at Alex letting him know that he didn't think Alex could do better than Jan. Alex chuckled. He agreed wholeheartedly. There was no one like Jan.

Alex had never felt that feeling before, but he knew what it was. He'd seen it in the eyes of his brother and Esme. He was falling in love with Jan.

Would she laugh when he told her? Maybe she'd knock him over the head with another rolling pin? It didn't matter. He'd take it. Just as long as she took him.

She'd been silent through the whole exchange. It was quite unlike her. Had she not liked the arrangement that the two men had set out for her? Was she simply biding her time to give him an earful? He turned to her, uncertain of what he would say. But she wasn't there.

"Where did she go?"

Esme and Leo looked over Alex's shoulder as though to confirm that Jan was no longer present. Alex did a complete three hundred sixty degree turn about the room. Jan wasn't hiding in any corners. As he came back around to face Leo and Esme, he saw it.

Tiny sparks of light went off in the distance. The

sparks were too big and frequent to be fireflies. He knew the press was out there, and then he realized what the bursts of light were.

"Oh, no," he muttered, taking off out of the room.

As he came out the front door, his suspicions were confirmed. Cameras flashed like an American Fourth of July fireworks display. The press stood behind the iron gates of the castle, pawing to get in like zombies looking for warm bodies. There was one solitary warm body making slow steps toward the gate.

Alex rushed to her. It didn't take him long to overtake her. Jan's steps were slow and uncertain. Lights flashed in her face. Reporters shouted at her. All the while, Jan resembled an actual deer caught in headlights.

He remembered her reaction the first time the press accosted her, as they made their way down a runway to their plane. They'd been lined up as though on two sides of an aisle as they stared and shouted questions at her. She'd gone catatonic under their scrutiny.

She wasn't quite catatonic now. Just a bundle of nerves. Without needing to be told, Alex understood the trauma she was reliving.

It was her wedding day all over again. She'd been left to face the crowd alone. But she wasn't alone. He was there with her. He'd always be by her side. And Leo and Esme were hot on his heels.

Jan was surrounded by the ones who loved her most. The ones who believed in her. The ones who'd never let her down or let her walk down an aisle alone.

She needed to know that. As she opened her mouth to speak, Alex stepped up. He wrapped an arm around her waist and pulled her into his warm body.

Jan startled. She turned and looked up at him, her gaze wide with surprise. In real time, Alex saw the tension release from the corners of her eyes. He saw her mouth relax as she let out a long, slow exhale.

As she leaned on him and took comfort and solace in his hold, Alex felt like the king of the world. "I have an announcement to make," he said, never taking his eyes off the woman he wanted to hold onto for the rest of his life.

All went silent. The reporters stopped questioning. The cameras stopped clicking. The pencils stopped scratching. Even the night crawlers hushed to hear what their prince had to say.

"Chef Peppers and I are opening a restaurant together. We will serve fusion fare of the likes your taste buds could never imagine. We will install hydroponics in the back of the garden for fresh fruits and vegetables. This is a tactic that I learned from my time in Nairobi where I helped locals to install the technology. Our restaurant, The Prince's Palette, will be entirely farm to table produce using recipes and spices I learned while helping cities install food co-ops and farmer's markets around the world. This venture will be successful because when this woman and I are in the kitchen together, magic happens."

A grin spread across Jan's face. She looked up at Alex

as though he'd hung the moon for her. Alex felt certain he could stretch that tall and reach the night's sky for this woman.

"And the wedding?" shouted a reporter. "The inheritance?"

Alex's gaze never left the woman he loved, the woman he wanted to spend the rest of his life with. "There's not going to be any wedding."

Jan blinked. Her bottom lip trembled, and she shut her eyes. Alex felt a shudder run through her body, and he pulled her closer into his heat.

"I don't need any collateral to secure my future with this woman," he said.

Jan opened her eyes and looked at him. They stared directly into each other's gazes. Alex felt she was seeing into his soul.

"I know with every fiber of my being that we will be partners for the rest of our life. And that that partnership will be fruitful, and bountiful, and filled with mutual respect and utter devotion and ... love."

Another tremble went through Jan's body. This time, it didn't have the tinge of sorrow. It was a shiver of delight.

Alex went down on one knee. He took Jan's hand in his. "Jan Peppers, will you do me the honor of never marrying me."

There was a confused silence that rippled through the crowd. Alex only had eyes for Jan. He saw when the true meaning of his words, meaning that only those in their circle would understand, hit her.

"Will you go on this journey through life with me with no safety net knowing that I believe in us and will do everything in my power to bring about our success?"

Jan opened her mouth, but no words would come out. After a few deep breaths, she tried again. "Yes, Alex. Yes, I'll never marry you."

Alex rose and scooped this magnificent woman into his arms. Jan was smart and witty and talented and his. "You know it's not just your cooking I love, don't you?"

"You know I'm not in it for your inheritance."

"Or the crown?" he asked

"Well …" She cocked her head as though considering. "A tiara is way cuter than a chef's hat."

"I'll give you a tiara."

"I'm good with your heart." She placed her hand over the beating organ to the right of his chest.

"You have it," he said.

"And you have mine," said Jan.

"What just happened?" one of the reporters asked. "Are they getting married or not?"

"Oh, they're definitely getting married," came Leo's commanding voice.

Alex was fine with that … one day. Perhaps in a year, after the restaurant, which he'd allow his brother to finance, was doing well. But for now, he pulled Jan into his arms and kissed her lightly. Then because he was a glutton, he deepened the kiss.

All around him, cameras flashed. But for once in his life, he didn't mind what story they printed in the papers because this particular headline could not be spun into any other tale except *a Prince in Love.*